For fourteen years now *Perry Rhodan* has been acknowledged to be the world's top-selling science fiction series. Originally published in magazine form in Germany, the series has now appeared in hardback and paperback in the States.

Over five hundred *Perry Rhodan* clubs exist on the Continent and *Perry Rhodan* fan conventions are held annually. The first Perry Rhodan film, *SOS From Outer Space*, has now been released in Europe.

The series has sold over 140 million copies in Europe alone

Also available in the *Perry Rhodan* series

Clark Darlton

PERRY RHODAN 19:

Mutants vs Mutants

Futura Publications Limited
An Orbit Book

An Orbit Book

First published in Great Britain in 1976
by Futura Publications Limited
Copyright © 1972 by Ace Books
An Ace Book by arrangement with Arthur Moewig Verlag
'Relics from the Earth' copyright 1930 by Gernsback
Publications Inc.
'Pursuit to Mars', originally copyrighted as 'Edison's
Conquest of Mars'; revised and edited version
copyrighted 1969, 1972 by Forrest J Ackerman.
'Little Johnny' copyright 1948 by Fantasy
Publishing Co Inc; courtesy of William L Crawford
and by arrangement with the author's agent.

DEDICATION
The English Edition is Dedicated to the late ROG PHILLIPS
who, among many other stories, wrote 'The Mutants' in 1946.

Series and characters created and directed by Karl-Herbert
Scheer and Walter Ernsting, translated by Wendayne
Ackerman and edited by Forrest J Ackerman.

ISBN: 0 8600 7922 8

Printed in Great Britain by
Richard Clay (The Chaucer Press), Ltd., Bungay, Suffolk

Futura Publications Limited
110 Warner Road, Camberwell, London SE5

1   DEATH OF A MUTANT

Captain Hawk was one of the most experienced space-pilot trainers. He sat now at the controls of training craft Z-82 and demonstrated to his two best pupils how even a big ship could swiftly avoid all obstacles.

The Z-82 was about 30 yards in length with room enough for just a three-man crew. It could attain the velocity of light-speed and was comparatively well-armed.

At barely 500 yards altitude the torpedo-shaped training ship of the Space Academy raced above the red desert areas of Mars and skilfully dodged the occasional mountaintops of the long mountain range.

Cadet Eberhardt sat to the left of his trainer and tried to absorb and retain the innumerable manipulation moves. Not that he was stupid – quite the contrary. But even he himself could not deny it was a fact that at times his comprehension was a bit slow. Not always – by no means – but usually just at a time when it really mattered. This was his only shortcoming.

To the right of Capt. Hawk sat another cadet. In contrast to Eberhardt he was slender, tall, almost skinny. Dark-brown hair crowned the upper half of his oval face in which two brown eyes were currently smiling gently and somewhat despondently. Cadet Julian Tifflor – Tiff to his friends and fellow students – knew almost subconsciously how to draw a heavy veil between himself and the world around him. Behind his dreaming eyes was hidden the energy of a miniature atom bomb. Despite his age – he had just turned 20 – Tiff was

5

a mathematical genius and a model of braveness and decision. He was one of the best students of the Space Academy.

Capt. Hawk pointed forward on a diagonal line. 'You see that mountaintop, gentlemen? Okay. I'll take the ship as close as possible to it without hitting it. Please — observe the reaction ability of Z-82 during this maneuver. Of course it isn't quite as great as out in open space because near to the ground we've the added use of atmospheric resistance as a brake.'

'Uh-huh,' said Eberhardt, nodding to Tiff, who for his part smiled quietly and placed his hands on the pseudo-controls in order to try to react at the same instant as the instructor. The electronic measuring instruments would exactly register and record each of his moves.

Eberhardt followed the example of his comrade.

The mountain peak raced closer. Indeed it looked as if the destroyer would slam full force into the bare reddish rocks but literally in the last second it shot past diagonally upwards into the dark blue sky in which the first stars were already visible.

'That was close,' commented cadet Eberhardt and leaned back. 'I don't think I'd ever attempt such a maneuver unless it was absolutely unavoidable.'

'You must learn to cope with any situation you might encounter,' admonished Captain Hawk as he looked at his wristwatch. 'It's time for us to return to Earth.'

'Yes,' agreed Tiff, lost in thought. 'I've asked for overnight leave.'

'While you are on duty you shouldn't think of your own funtime, cadet Tifflor. There's still a difficult flight back home ahead of us.'

'Those few miserable miles!' replied Tifflor scornfully. 'We'll make it in less than half an hour with this Z-82.'

'I don't plan to accelerate to the speed of light, although we could do that easily with our ship. We'll land at Nevada Fields in three hours.'

But Captain Hawk was wrong this time, though he couldn't foresee this of course. If only he had listened to Tiff's plea for a fast flight home everything might have turned out quite different and the events of the following days would have perhaps developed along other lines.

'Do you have all the calculations?' asked Hawk. 'We're assuming that our navigational robot is out of order and you must determine the fastest route to Earth. Without instruments. Here from this point. How long will you need for that?'

Tiff sighed and looked around. He noticed Mars, which meanwhile had shrunk to a size that filled exactly the spacecraft's observation window over on his side. The planet swiftly grew smaller. He saw clearly the network of the canals which in reality were no canals but low-lying valleys with sparse vegetation. There the roots grew down deep enough to reach as far as the meager supplies of ground water.

In the middle of the front window stood the blue earth. A tiny celestial body he could hardly recognize as his home planet. No wonder Tiff was sighing a bit despondently and shrugging his shoulders.

'Of course calculating our course isn't that simple but it can be done. But I don't think it will even be necessary to bother with it. Our present speed allows us to navigate by direct sight.'

Captain Hawk began to gesticulate angrily. 'Cadet Tifflor, don't forget you're here on a training ship! I am fully aware we could navigate by direct sight but that isn't the point here. I want to find out if you can also orient yourself in an unknown area of space without instruments. So get going, start calculating!'

Tiff threw a melancholy glance toward the constantly

shrinking planet Mars and noticed suddenly that the picture in the ship's observation port hole over on his side began to change. Earth, too, vanished from the front window, moved rapidly over to the side and out of his sight entirely. Hawk let the Z-82 'run wild,' so that the task Tiff had to solve would be more difficult.

That, too, he shouldn't have done but who can foresee what the future will bring? Anyhow, Captain Hawk didn't know it. The Z-82 was rushing through space with constant acceleration. Automatic gravity fields compensated for any change in flight direction or acceleration, so that the three-man crew didn't suffer from sudden increases or decreases in G's.

Eberhardt watched, full of pity, how Tiff started jotting numbers on a piece of paper. Captain Hawk reclined at ease in his chair, letting the space vehicle race into space without paying any attention to the course. Soon it would be his pupil's task to set the ship on the right course again and later on to bring it in for a safe landing at Nevada Fields.

Nobody observed the instruments.

Nobody except Eberhardt.

Unfortunately, this is where his slow reactions took their toll again. Compared to any normal Earthman—this should be emphasized at this point—he reacted quite quickly. Only when compared to the average space pilot did he not quite measure up.

Thus it took a full 10 seconds for him to become aware of the deflection of the sensor needle. This sensor was an instrument which constantly was sending out radar waves in all directions and then would register any reflexes that might occur. Such reflexes in empty space were extremely rare considering the relatively limited range of the instrument. They would only occur if asteroids or larger meteors were passing close by the ship – or when the spacecraft happened to be in their vicinity.

Cadet Eberhardt extended his arm and pointed to the tiny screen above the sensor's dial. 'There's something here,' he stated perplexed. 'Quite a good-sized chunk.'

With great effort Captain Hawk returned to a halfway sitting position. Then he stared spellbound at the instrument. An almost round spot was floating on the tiny screen. The spot grew rapidly in size as it came nearer to the training ship. With one jolt Captain Hawk came back to a completely upright position. His eyes swiftly took in the data on the dial. Then he shook his head. 'A destroyer ... Impossible. We're the only destroyer between Earth and Mars. Unless we change our direction he'll be almost upon us in a few seconds. Now, he's slowing down. Strange!'

By now the slender form of the sister ship had become visible to the naked eye. It was looping in a broad sweep and approached once more, but this time from in front of the Z-82.

'Maybe the New Power has ...' began Tiff, but Captain Hawk shook his head.

'According to the last radio message we received from the Academy, Perry Rhodan has no other destroyers at present out in space. We are the only ones. If I didn't know so well this type of ship ...'

But he couldn't manage to complete his sentence and reveal to his two pupils what then would be the case.

A blinding flash came from in front of them. An almost orange-colored light-ray leapt from the nose of the other destroyer and sped faster than the human eye could follow toward the Z-82.

Captain Hawk didn't react fast enough and also Tiff was taken by surprise by this sudden attack. Although he bent over to the left and slammed his fist on the lever, still the energy envelope enveloped them just the fraction of a second too late.

Fortunately for them, the pilot of the other destroyer turned out to be a miserable shot. That is fortunately for the Z-82 but this luck did not include Captain Hawk.

The hostile energy ray didn't pierce the hull of the training ship's nose but it was as if the ship had run into a solid wall. Even the G's neutralizers couldn't help them out any longer. The force of the sudden impact hurled Captain Hawk out of his seat and threw him violently, head forward, against the control panel of the navigator brain.

Tiff, too, was jerked forward, but he managed to brake the sudden impact with his outstretched hands. He sprained both wrists, though he didn't notice this at all at the moment.

Cadet Eberhardt had more luck than sense. He was the only one to have fastened his safety belt – something everyone neglected as a rule. Although the safety belt almost rent him in two, it nevertheless saved him from sharing Hawk's fate. For by the time it would have occurred to Eberhardt to stretch out his arms and brake his fall forward, at least another two and a half seconds would have elapsed. And that would simply have been too long.

Tiff took in with once glance that his trainer was dead. His skull had been smashed by the impact against the control panel. But there was no time now to worry about the dead man. There were far more urgent things he had to do first – far more important.

After the apparently unsuccessful attack the other ship had made a turn and set out again for a frontal attack. With one leap Tiff swung himself into the now empty seat of the trainer and took over the controls. He moved out of the way by curving sharply to the right, accelerated and went over to attack the unkown enemy. All the while the wildest ideas were coursing through his brain.

Who was the pilot of the attacking destroyer? It couldn't be anybody from the Space Academy, that was totally unthinkable. And that a ship of the New Power was attempting to shoot down their own spacecraft was just as unlikely.

But who else could it be?

Tiff had no idea that Perry Rhodan's greatest enemy had stolen three destroyers and had now proceeded to man them with his weak-willed tools who had been ordered to shoot on sight anything that was part of the New Power.

Of course, Tiff hadn't the slightest inkling of this. All he knew was that some unknown person or persons had attacked him with a ship so familiar to him that they had almost finished him off. To try his luck by taking flight made no sense, for the enemy would simply accelerate to the same speed as the Z-82. Besides it was quite against Tiff's nature to take to his heels and leave behind an unsolved riddle.

The hostile ship didn't react especially fast. Tiff steered his craft around and with an almost elegant loop succeeded in pointing the Z-82's nose directly at the flaming rear of the unknown destroyer. This was the only spot – as Tiff knew theoretically – where the destroyer was vulnerable, for there was some kind of a hole in the protective energy screen to prevent the drive's pulse rays from rebounding onto the ship.

Tiff's eyes searched for and found the red lever of the neutron gun. All throughout the many hours of flight training he had never been permitted to even touch that legendary lever, let alone depress it. It was supposed to be used only in case of dire emergency, as Captain Hawk kept stressing, for this lever would activate a death-deal-

11

ing weapon whose effect ...

This emergency was now at hand.

Cadet Tifflor no longer felt bound by any rules and regulations. He was acting now in self-defense.

The enemy craft's rear came nearer as Z-82 increased its speed. Then the hostile spaceship seemed to veer away to one side. With lightning speed Tiff grasped the red lever and simultaneously pushed down on it.

One second.

Two seconds.

The orange-colored finger of energy shot out of his destroyer's nose and penetrated the flaming drive-rays of the hostile spacecraft. With a velocity close to the speed of light the energy finger bored into the jets and advanced as far as the engine room, devouring everything along its way until it reached the Arkonide reactor.

Three seconds later Tiff let go of the red lever and pulled his destroyer sharply around. With incredible speed – it seemed as if both ships were standing still – Tiff's destroyer swept close past his opponent's damaged vessel.

Fascinated, Tiff observed the effect of his neutron ray bombardment.

At first a hole became visible at the rear of the other destroyer, then the edges of the hole began to burn. A wreath of fire enveloped the ship's rear. A force released by a sudden and noiseless explosion then extinguished the ring of fire. The ship's rear broke apart and some invisible force hurled its wreckage in all directions. The ship's interior seemed to break loose, apparently endeavoring to separate from the rest. Now the outer hull ripped apart. The strong metal wall bent and crumpled as if it were made of tinfoil.

The destroyer broke in two, right through the middle.

The enemy had been practically destroyed.

Tiff heaved a sigh of relief. Only then did he find time to look after his trainer and his fellow student.

Captain Hawk was lying collapsed in a heap between the pilot's seat and the front wall. There was no doubt that he was dead. Nevertheless, Tiff checked for the presence of any vital signs, but there weren't any. Cadet Eberhardt, who had been silently sitting next to Tifflor, unable to do anything, was slowly recovering from his shock. His first remark was typical for him. 'Now we are without our instructor. How will we get back to Earth?'

Tiff repressed his anger. 'Eberhardt, aren't you overlooking that we have quite a few hours of training behind us? Besides, I've already calculated our flight course. We'll be landing on Earth in two hours. Now, will you help me bring Captain Hawk back to his cabin?'

They placed their dead trainer on his cot and covered him up. He would be laid to his final rest in his small hometown back on Terra. His students however would never forget him, when later on they would roam through the wide expanses of space as the brave commanders of their proud ships, for whatever they were and knew they owed to him – Captain Hawk.

The rudderless nose of the hostile spaceship had moved only very slightly over to the side. Later on it would drift off into the asteroid belt.

Tiff narrowed his eyes and examined the wreck.

Its front part was undamaged but the other side, where it had been rent apart, resembled a rubble heap. Molten panels of the cabin and half-way vaporized metal plates of the hull jutted out from among the jagged edges. Nearby drifted bent and crumpled pieces whose origin and purpose were no longer recognizable.

But amidst this wreckage there might still remain an undamaged cabin in which the unknown foe were locked in helplessly. Perhaps they were still armed with hand

13

weapons but they could use these of course only if one were to penetrate their sealed space tombs.

And this was exactly what Tiff had in mind. He said to Eberhardt: 'Let's have a look at those fellows who wanted to send us to hell.'

And he started to steer the Z-82 close to the wreck. He glanced significantly at the built-in small cabinet, looked at the remote controls and murmured: 'Somebody ought to climb into his pressurized spacesuit now and leave our ship through the airlock to pay a visit over there and look around.'

'Sure,' agreed Eberhardt. 'That would be a splendid idea.'

Tiff was waiting. But he waited in vain. For there was nothing else that Eberhardt intended adding to his remark. The subject had been sufficiently explored for his taste.

'I'm glad you agree. This somebody will be you, my friend. Get going; climb into your spacesuit and transfer to the wreck over there. Take along one of our ray guns in case the doors are stuck.'

'Why me?' Eberhardt's eyes took on the size and shape of small saucers. 'I'm supposed to leave our ship? All alone? And then clear out that band of gangsters? Listen, cadet Tifflor, I'm a space pilot not an FBI agent.'

'*Commander* Tifflor, if you please,' corrected Tiff and assumed a most official-looking mien. 'And hurry up for a change!'

Eberhardt shrugged his shoulders, rose slowly from his seat and took a pulse-ray gun from the weapon cabinet on the wall. All the training ships of the Academy were equipped with this absolutely fatal weapon, built according to an Arkonide principle. He threw a last desperate glance at Tiff, waited in vain for a sign of compassion and finally moved over to the door. There he stopped.

14

'I'll finish off that gang and avenge Hawk,' he said triumphantly. 'I'll do it, all by myself. And what will you do, Tiff?'

'I'll make sure that nothing untoward will befall you meanwhile,' Tiff reassured him as cool as a cucumber and pointed to the red lever of the neutron cannon. 'At least I'll try to do my best, I promise.'

Eberhardt swallowed hard and without further comment left the cabin. Tiff waited until the green control light lit up before he started the process of depressurizing and vacuumizing the airlock.

The Z-82 was now hovering apparently without motion about 30 feet next to the wreck. Once Tiff believed for a moment he'd seen some movement behind one of the dark bull's-eyes of the cabin but this might have been just an optical illusion. But no, there it was again! He could clearly make out the outlines of a human figure. A weak light flared up. Of course there could be no electric current over there and they had to make do with weak batteries. Provided they had any besides their flashlights. Their radio installation had also been destroyed by the detonation.

A red light began to glow on the front panel near Tiff. The airlock had been pumped empty and Eberhardt had opened the exit hatch. Similar abandon-ship maneuvers in deep space had been practiced many times by them but this time it was for real. And besides, nobody could know what dangers might be lurking over there in the wreck. It was quite possible that the pirates – that's what the unknown enemy were considered to be by Tiff – had their own pressurized spacesuits with them in their cabin.

Now Eberhardt became visible. He was floating, attached to a thin line, close in front of Tiff as he slowly approached the rotating wreck. The shadow behind the window hatch of the broken-off nose of the formerly hostile spaceship seemed suddenly to freeze. He too must have caught sight of Eberhardt.

Eberhardt braked gently as he landed on the hull of the wreck. Cautiously he moved ahead until he reached the window hatch. He peered inside and saw the face of a man who stared at him with wide open, horror-filled eyes.

The stranger was wearing a spacesuit, however his helmet was not closed. His dark skin indicated he might be a mulatto but Eberhardt wasn't quite sure. In any case he was filled with deep satisfaction when he could clearly recognize the fear expressed in the other's face.

He nodded grimly toward the man and showed him his pulse-ray gun, just to make sure. Then he crept carefully toward the torn-up part of the nose. A glance sufficed for Eberhardt to determine that he had in front of him a corridor which led to the various cabins of the ship. By some miracle the door to the command center had remained untouched.

What now?

He wanted to seize the unknown foe alive, for nobody would be helped by his death. For they were naturally most interested to find out who their opponents were and who was hiding behind this incomprehensible attack. Therefore Eberhardt grasped his raygun and knocked with it against the door. Three times.

Of course he couldn't hear anything for there was no air to conduct the sound. But the person inside the cabin could hear the knock at the door.

Eberhardt leaned his helmetted head against the door. If the unknown should knock against it, in turn the vibrations would be transferred to the air inside his helmet. Hardly 10 seconds had passed when he heard three knocks. That could only mean they were ready to negotiate.

Eberhardt thanked his fate that he had always paid attention during their radio training. He remembered the sarcastic remarks which many of his fellow students couldn't help uttering when they had to learn the Morse alphabet. Why bother learning the Morse code in an era when there existed direct audio-visual communication over distances spanning interplanetary space?

Well, at this moment he realized suddenly why they had been bothered with such antiquated trifles.

Almost automatically he replied and knocked out a message in Morse code:

Close your helmet and open the door a bit. Come out backwards. Unarmed. I am waiting.

There was no answer but a minute later the door opened. There was a rush of air as it escaped through the opened cabin door. It almost dragged Eberhardt with it but he held fast to one of the twisted stays. In his right hand he held his pulse-ray gun, ready to shoot, pointed at the chink in the door.

First he saw an arm that cautiously groped backwards, then appeared the back of a spacesuit. It was the same type as worn by the cadets of the Academy. Therefore he had also ...

Eberhardt cursed himself because he hadn't at once thought of it. With a quick movement he flipped on his miniaturized radio installation. The other fellow might have switched his own on for quite some time already.

Sure enough, it was the case.

'... kind enough to bring me back to Mars.'

Eberhardt was startled. To Mars? He wanted to be brought back to Mars? He was coming from Mars in the first place? What was going on up there?

'Turn around and raise your hands!'

The stranger obeyed. Now Eberhardt could clearly see his face. He hadn't been mistaken earlier: he was a mulatto. His English was fluent.

'Where is the rest of the crew?' inquired Eberhardt.

Eberhardt was stunned to hear the stranger tell him: 'I am alone here.'

The man was unarmed, this was obvious at first glance. Eberhardt requested him to step aside and wait. Then he entered the command center of the wreck and convinced himself that it was indeed empty. Amazing, but the fellow must have flown the ship all alone. Strange.

Eberhardt left the command center and noticed with satisfaction that the other man hadn't budged from the spot.

'Get going! Float ahead! You see the open hatch over there? Get in. No nonsense. I have you covered with my weapon.'

The stranger didn't reply but took off from the wreck with a slight push. In a weightless state he floated across the bottomless abyss and landed somewhat to one side of the opening in the Z-82's hull. A slight move and he stood inside the airlock and waited.

Eberhardt followed him with mixed feelings. As far as he was concerned all proceeded too easily here. The stranger must realize that he was going to be faced with rather unpleasant alternatives. Why did he let everything happen without any resistance?

Tiff awaited the prisoner in the command center. He waited patiently until the mulatto had unscrewed his helmet. Then he studied his face. It made a surprisingly honest impression. There was a trace of astonishment in his eyes, fear and indecision. Now a bit of defiance was added. His lips were tightly pressed on each other. His chin was thrust out energetically, revealing great vitality, but this was in obvious contradiction to how the man seemed to resign himself to his fate.

'Do you speak English?' asked Tiff and motioned to

Eberhardt to close the door leading to the corridor.

The mulatto nodded but didn't say a word.

'Who are you?'

Again no answer.

'You've attacked us without provocation,' continued Tiff, feeling his anger rising. Now he was boiling with fury when he remembered his dead instructor Captain Hawk. 'I want to know in whose behalf you were acting and why you did it!'

'I'm not permitted to speak,' mumbled the mulatto and closed his lips tight as if he wanted to prevent an indiscreet remark from slipping past his lips.

'What? You aren't permitted to speak?' Tiff's thoughts were buzzing and tumbling in his brain. Maybe they had accidentally happened onto something really important. He no longer believed he was confronted here with a simple case of piracy. After all, what treasures could anyone hope to find on one of the training ships of the Space Academy?

'As you wish. Then other things will make you talk. Cadet Eberhardt, lock the man in a cell and take away his helmet. Pump all air out of the antechamber so that any attempted flight will be absolutely impossible.'

Tifflor watched as the prisoner let himself be taken away, disinterested as if all this was of no concern to him. Tiff waited until Eberhardt returned and confirmed that their prisoner was safely locked up in his cell.

'Set course for Terra!' decided Tiff. 'Get in touch with the Central Command and report the incident. I suppose they'll be interested to hear about it.'

And while the Z-82 was shooting out into space with incredible acceleration, leaving the drifting wreck behind to its fate, the radio waves rushed ahead of them. Eberhardt described all the details of the assault, reported the tragic death of Captain Hawk and was deeply astonished when he was suddenly interrupted by an especially powerful sender. An excited voice inquired: 'What did the ship look like that attacked you?'

Eberhardt reacted surprisingly quick. 'It was a destroyer of the same type. We are at a loss to explain the incident.'

'And you took a prisoner?'

'Yes, we did. Will you please identify yourself!' added Eberhardt as an afterthought.

'Security Center of the New Power, Reginald Bell.'

'Of course, the Security Center. It's got ears all over the place.'

'Thank Heavens!' countered Bell and added: 'Stay tuned in. I must transmit this message. It may be that Perry Rhodan will get in touch with you directly.'

There was a clicking sound in the loudspeaker, followed by a humming. A bit surprised, Eberhardt turned to Tiff: 'Reginald Bell! He has his nose into everything.'

Tiff in turn now demonstrated how fast he too could adjust to this new situation. With a last glance at the control panel he punched for automatic guidance which would keep the destroyer on its course. He got up and stepped over to Eberhardt's seat at the commu-set.

'I'm taking over,' he said with nonchalance. 'We'll soon find out what they want from us. Watch the sensors, we don't want to be surprised a second time. I've a feeling that something isn't the way it's supposed to be.'

Little did he know how correct he was in that assumption.

*   *   *

When the first manned atomic rocket landed safely on the Moon, nobody suspected that a new chapter in the history of mankind had begun. Major Rhodan, the commander of the expedition, met on the Moon the Arkonides, a humanoid race ruling a star realm from their home planet Arkon, some 34,000 light-years away. Rhodan came to the rescue of the stranded Arkonides and they expressed their gratitude by letting him share in the extensive knowledge of a race that had already known space travel for thousands of years.

Helped by the Arkonides, Perry Rhodan founded the New Power on Earth, prevented the atomic war and was now endeavoring to finally unite the whole world. His headquarters: the city of Terrania in the middle of the Gobi Desert. Terrania – the most modern metropolis on the globe, containing the marvels of a technology and knowledge many thousands of years old. If necessary, the city could be closed off from the outside world by erecting an energy dome around and above itself. An army of 10,000 soldiers and robots were in charge of the New Power's security.

The Minister of Security, Reginald Bell, one of the men who had accompanied Rhodan on the first mission to the Moon, waited patiently till the six-foot-high picture screen lit up on the wall. A writing desk became visible. A man was sitting behind it. Very haggard, his dark-blond hair combed straight back, narrow steel-gray eyes alight with an inner fire. Although Perry Rhodan was already 44 years old, he still gave the appearance of being just 38. And he would never look a day older for the inconceivable knowledge of a race long since extinct had rendered him almost immortal. Every six decades he had to visit again the planet of Eternal Life, where that mysterious biological cell shower was located which would bestow another 60 years of youth on him.

Reginald Bell also had been on the planet Wanderer and he too had been treated for conservation of his cells.

'One of the stolen destroyers has shown up again, Perry,' said Bell. His eyes were sparkling with pent-up

21

excitement. 'It's attacked one of our training ships from the Academy!'

Perry Rhodan's eyebrows shot upward. 'Where was that?'

'In the vicinity of Mars. Luckily, one of the cadets showed enough presence of mind to wipe out the enemy after their instructor had been killed during the attack. The cadet also made one prisoner.'

Perry Rhodan's face lit up with sudden interest. 'A prisoner?'

'Yes, that's why I'm reporting this incident to you. I thought you might like to have a look at the fellow.'

'I bet you'd like that too, Reg! 'Where's prisoner now?'

'He's still locked up in a cell of the training ship Z-82. Wait a minute! I'll connect you with the destroyer, then you can talk directly with the young cadet. The ship's on its way back to Earth.'

A few seconds later Cadet Tifflor came on. He described once again in a clear precise manner the recent events. Then he waited while Perry Rhodan absorbed and pondered what he just had heard. Shortly Rhodan inquired: 'What's your name?'

'Cadet Julian Tifflor, sir?'

'Cadet Tifflor, you will land on the spaceport of Terrania and then report to me in person. I'll inform your superior officer back at the Academy of this change in plan. Keep a very close eye on your prisoner! He is of the utmost importance to us. The body of Captain Hawk will be transported to his home town. At what time may I expect you?'

'In 80 minutes, sir.'

Tifflor's voice was filled with respect and high esteem. Perry Rhodan was for him not only the chief of the Space Academy but even more so a distant legendary figure. Where would the world be now if Rhodan hadn't succeeded in harnessing the might of the Arkonides for the benefit of mankind? The inhabitants of Earth might have annihilated each other long since and our world no longer exist at all.

'Very well, Cadet Tifflor, I'll expect to see you then.'

Bell broke off the connection and instructed the military posts to let the Z-82 come in undisturbed for a landing in about 80 minutes and to bring its crew immediately to the Ministry of Defense in Terrania. Then Bell turned to Perry, whose lifelike image was still visible on the picture screen on the wall. 'Well, what do you think?'

'It's undoubtedly one of the three destroyers stolen by the mutant master.'

'Mutant master, that's all I hear!' grumbled Bell. 'If we only knew who's behind that name? A supermutant? A monster?'

'Regardless what — he's a very clever person who's determined to become the next New Power on Earth. It won't be easy to prevent him from doing so. So far we've been unable to find out the identity of our opponent, we only know that we are dealing with an extraordinarily intelligent, unscrupulous foe who shies away from nothing, not even murder.'

'We'll interrogate the prisoner and get all the information we need about the great unknown enemy. We'll get him yet!'

'Provided our prisoner will cooperate with us,' warned Rhodan.

'Don't worry about that, he'll cooperate. And besides, we have André Noir to assist us.'

'I wasn't thinking so much of his own resistance,' Rhodan said. 'I was more concerned that the mutant master might have made sure our prisoner *can't* provide us with any information, not even if we try to force him under hypnosis.'

23

'That remains to be seen,' replied Bell, always ready shoo away his own doubts.

*   *   *

It was a great moment for Tiff when he first stood before Perry Rhodan. He was overawed to be in the presence of the savior of mankind, the idol of modern youth, the legendary Perry Rhodan who had repelled the invasion of the Mind Snatchers and the Topides and who had saved mankind from destruction.

Perry Rhodan greeted him with a smile.

This was probably the greatest surprise in Tiff's whole life and later on he admitted to himself that he was somewhat disappointed by it at first.

Next to Rhodan stood another man whom the cadet recognized from many photos and television broadcasts: Reginald Bell, The Minister of Security of the New Power and also Rhodan's best friend. Bell also smiled but it was an impatient and demanding smile.

Tiff stood at attention. 'Cadet Tifflor and Cadet Eberhardt back from a training flight. Special incidents to report: attack by a destroyer, Captain Hawk killed in action, enemy craft desroyed, one prisoner taken.'

Rhodan's smile vanished now as he stepped closer to Tiff and shook his hand. 'Thank you for your determination and presence of mind, Cadet Tifflor. You have avenged Captain Hawk and rendered us a great service besides. If it hadn't been for you we would still be in the dark on who is responsible for making space unsafe with our stolen destroyers. Is that your prisoner?'

Eberhardt and the mulatto stood half a step behind Tiff. Apart from their different colored complexion there was no difference between the two for both were still wearing the light-pressurized spacesuit without their helmets. And in the Academy for the training of space pilots

24

there is no racial discrimination.

Therefore it was nothing unusual when Rhodan pointed at Eberhardt, who was standing, with a deeply embarrassed smile, next to his prisoner. Tiff tried to suppress an overwhelming desire to laugh out loud. He grinned broadly as he corrected Rhodan. 'Pardon me, sir, but *this* is Cadet Eberhardt, who overwhelmed the survivor of the wrecked enemy ship and took him prisoner.'

Rhodan shook Eberhardt's hand. 'Then this must be the man,' he remarked and carefully examined the mulatto. He advanced toward him. 'Who are you? On whose behalf are you acting?'

No answer.

Bell, who had also welcomed and shaken hands with the two cadets frowned darkly. 'Let's skip the formalities; he isn't going to cooperate. Let's get our mutants! It won't take long for John Marshall to find out what's going on in this man's mind.'

Rhodan nodded in agreement. 'Take charge of the confrontation with our telepaths. I'll have a talk meanwhile with our guests here. As soon as the prisoner starts talking, let me know.'

Bell approached the mulatto and stared in the man's expressionless eyes, shook his head in despair and took him by the elbow. Arm in arm both left the room like two good friends. Pensively, Rhodan followed them with his eyes. Then he turned to Tiff.

'And now I'd like to hear a detailed account of what has taken place. I'd like to know all the details even if they seem insignificant to you. There must be some clue in all of this to what we're looking for.'

*   *   *

The presence of radioactivity in the Earth's atmosphere since the first atom bomb in 1945 had produced side effects much faster than scientists first had suspected. New mutants were constantly born without anybody being aware of this gradual change in man's former limitations. Then it was suddenly discovered that a number of apparently normal human beings possessed extraordinary abilities. There were telepaths and telekineticists. A man disappeared in Africa and reappeared the same second 1800 miles away: he had teleported himself across this distance. Another man could receive radio messages without the intermediary of a radio set. The human brain all of a sudden displayed abilities that had never before been known to exist. Everywhere on Earth mutants began to pop up. Only a few of them possessed positive changes. As long as they remained isolated from each other, they represented no danger to mankind but united in a well-organized force they could become a remarkably effective army.

Rhodan had realized this soon enough. He sent out a special search commando to all parts of the world, especially to Japan where the first atom bomb had been detonated. It took only a few months till the mutant corps of the New Power organized. This corps formed the backbone of Rhodan's pacifistic forces.

John Marshall was one of these mutants. Thanks to his telepathic gift he made unnecessary any further reliance on even the best lie detector. No thought remained hidden from his probing mind and he had found out that he could communicate even with extraterrestrial beings.

The prisoner, however, was just a normal human being – at least this was the impression he gave. When John Marshall tried to penetrate his thoughts he met no obstacle. But all he encountered were merely superficial thoughts.

'Who gave you the order to attack the training ship

26

Z-82?' asked John Marshall and gazed into the mulatto's eyes. Bell was standing next to Marshall, trying to put on especially grim airs. But the prisoner seemed not to notice. He started to give an answer but something prevented him from uttering a single word. Evidently he wanted to reply but was unable to do so.

Ishy Matsu, the Japanese girl telepath, had concentrated more intensely because she was expecting some difficulties. 'He has a hypno-block,' she whispered. 'His memories seem to be imbedded in a kind of a hypnotic energy field. We cannot pierce it.'

'How about applying a counter-block?' suggested Bell.

Ishy shook her head. 'I doubt it'll work but we can always try. André Noir would be the right person for this task.'

Noir, a Frenchman, born in Japan, entered the room a few minutes later. He stopped near the door. He regarded the prisoner in an inconspicuous manner. Noir was the so called 'hypno' of the mutant corps. He was capable of penetrating effortlessly into the consciousness of every living creature and to bring it under his will. No one would have suspected that this man, who looked so easy-going, was the most powerful hypnotist in the world. So far he had proven to be infallible.

André Noir approached slowly. His eyes were fixed on the prisoner's face. Without looking at Marshall or Bell he said: 'You may tell us your name without fear for you are here among friends. Also give us the name of the person who charged you with this mission. I know you are being forced to act via hypnotic compulsion but you must help me to remove this force, otherwise you'll never be a free man again.'

'I'd rather live and be subjected to this force than not live at all,' said the prisoner, hesitating. Everybody pres-

27

ent felt clearly that these words were put in his mouth by someone else.

'It's better to live as a free man,' said Noir with emphasis.

The prisoner did not react in response to his command.

Noir applied his tremendous mind powers to crack and shatter the ring an unknown person had placed around the conscious mind of the mulatto. John Marshall and Bell waited, silently. The tiny, delicate Japanese girl's face looked like a mask: she was capable of following the procedure in all details.

Almost unnoticed someone else had entered the half-darkened room. He remained near the door.

Perry Rhodan.

And then the block was broken. The prisoner suddenly opened his eyes wide, stared at the man across the room from him, seemed totally bewildered and began to utter sounds.

At first incomprehensible, the sounds tumbled over his lips, hastily, as if uttered in terrible fear. And then suddenly he spoke English: '... attack everything and destroy it ... hatred, horrible hatred ... to rule the world ... mutants ... me too ... the mutant master ...'

'Who is the mutant master?' shouted Rhodan from the door. He stepped closer and peered into the prisoner's eyes. Noir desperately shook his head and raised his arm imploringly as if he were trying to hold back Perry Rhodan.

'The mutant master ...' stammered the prisoner. 'The supermutant is ...'

His face changed with frightening speed. The prisoner seemed to perceive something horrifying and inconceivable. A pain visibly raced through his body. His legs gave slowly under him Rhodan lept to his side, trying to catch him. Marshall, too, attempted to help. André Noir,

28

however, did nothing of the sort; he merely retreated a few steps.

'It's too late,' Noir murmured. 'The hypno-block was far too powerful. But he wasn't killed by the hypno-block. He simply was obeying an overpowering hypnotic command.'

They laid the stilled figure of the mulatto on a couch. John Marshall bent over in order to examine him.

'A hypnotic command?' asked Rhodan and looked at Noir. 'Who gave him that command?'

'That I couldn't say but I'd guess it came from the mutant master.'

'And what kind of an order would he have issued to that poor fellow?'

'To die! He simply ordered him to die on the spot. And our prisoner obeyed.'

'Is that possible?'

The Frenchman's face grew somber. 'I believe I've found my match. The unknown supermutant has outdistanced me by far.'

And without waiting for a reply, Noir left the room. Bell, who had been standing the while very quietly in a corner of the room, now walked over to Perry Rhodan. 'Once again that mutant master! Now we have additional proof. He *is* a monster! He's murdered two people within the last two hours: first Captain Hawk and now one of his own men.'

'He's giving orders to those mutants that he has in his power,' said Marshall. 'The instant our prisoner was dying I managed to penetrate his mind for just a second. He was a weak mutant and had a photographic memory. This enabled him to fly the destroyer all alone. I'm sure he could have told us quite a few things of interest.'

'Right,' agreed Rhodan. 'That's exactly why he had to die.' He frowned and looked at Marshall. 'Couldn't you determine from which direction the hypnotic influence originated?'

'From which direction? What do you mean by that?'

'Well, if this supermutant kept our prisoner under personal surveillance, then his hypno impulses must have come from the same direction. I hoped you'd be able to tell me.'

'Noir was puzzled by exactly the same question when he left the room. He wondered why the impulses were coming from two directions. Exactly from the west and the east.'

Rhodan seemed startled by this revelation. '*Simultaneously* from two directions? Odd! But maybe not that strange after all – the Earth *is* round. But I could have bet that they were coming from one and the same direction: above. Or is Mars still below the horizon?'

John Marshall didn't say a word. He kept following Rhodan with his eyes as the latter left the room.

Bell pointed to the motionless figure lying on the couch. 'So he's dead?'

'Yes,' said Marshall softly.

2 'I HAVE MET THE SUPERMUTANT'

Lieutenant Becker was in charge of the East border station. It consisted of 10 observation posts positioned at regular short intervals and equipped with Arkonide neutron cannons. These stations were manned at all times. The border guards had their quarters on flat terrain. A small movie house, a bar and a swimming pool were the only diversions for the men out here in this isolated spot.

Sergeant Harras and his men had just returned to their base from their period of guard duty. Harras had dismissed the men, who were now off duty for eight hours. By the time they would have to report to their posts again it would already be dark.

It was a very hot day, the sun seemingly burning everything to a crisp. Not a cloud was to be seen in the sky. Harras couldn't think of anything better than to get out of his sweaty uniform as fast as possible and take a running jump in the swimming pool. He planned to stay in the cool water until hunger would force him out and he'd stroll over to the cafeteria for a hearty meal.

He put on his swim trunks and left the room which he shared with two other sergeants, strolled across the lawn and stopped at the edge of the swimming pool. He breathed the vitalizing scent of the water in which some 30 men were frolicking about, apparently forgetting that in reality they were here in the middle of a desert. They jostled and joked with each other and didn't spare Harras either.

'You afraid?' somebody close by hollered and hit the surface of the water so skilfully with the flat of his hand that Harras was showered by a sudden water spout. 'Get in, get in! What are you waiting for in that hot sun!'

Sergeant Harras hesitated. Just one second ago he had looked forward to jumping right into the cool water. But now something held him back. Still, his desire to cool off in the water was stronger than all vague dark fears. He advanced one step and lept into the water.

'The pool is running over!' called somebody in mock horror. Harras couldn't hear it. He let himself drift down to the bottom of the pool and was glad not to have to hear any more intruding voices. For a moment he felt grateful to fate for this brief solitude.

Strange desires and thoughts began to possess him and tuned out his normal ego. Somewhere in his head he felt a peculiar pressure. He had palpitations of the heart. Maybe he was holding his breath too long?

He kicked his legs against the bottom of the pool and rose to the surface. He looked around the swimming pool and what he saw seemed to confirm his dark and incomprehensible feelings of foreboding. All his comrades were eagerly swimming toward the edge of the basin and scrambling on land. Nobody spoke a word and it was as if they all had received a command during the short time he had been submerged in the water. And the command must have told them to get out of the water immediately.

Over on the other side, at the exit door of the barracks, Lieutenant Becker came into view. He was waving both his arms and shouting something. Harras could not understand what he was saying. Nevertheless he knew what Becker had called out: 'Alarm! Report immediately! Battle gear!'

Sergeant Harras ran to his room, quickly put back on his uniform, made sure he had his hand raygun and rushed to the exercise yard. Half the company was already assembled there. From the direction of the boundary station they could see some caterpillar track vehicles approaching. Harras was dumbfounded to see that they had removed the neutron ray cannons from the gun emplacements at the border. They had been mounted instead on the vehicles. That meant the border was left without protection. Perhaps the worker robots might take over guard duty from now on.

Lieutenant Becker apparently wasn't worried at all that his platoons had not reported to a man. He seemed to be extremely nervous and fidgety and kept urging his rank and file to hurry up. Hardly had the 10 armored tanks lined up in formation than he gave the signal to leave.

Sergeant Harras had an uneasy feeling that something wasn't the way it was supposed to be but he couldn't pull himself together sufficiently to systematically think about the latest events. The pressure in his head had not diminished; on the contrary it had become worse. Something indefinable forced him to set himself in motion.

Lieutenant Becker's column advanced toward the spaceship assembly halls and hangars of the New Power which were located about one mile away inside the actual barred area. Their barrels lowered, the neutron ray cannons led the column. The gunners sat at the controls, ready to shoot.

For a fleeting moment Harras intended to ask his neighbor what actually had taken place but when he saw the man's pencil-thin lips he dismissed the thought. Something horrible must have happened.

But no, that was sheer nonsense what they were doing . . .

His attention was diverted at this point. From the direction of the hangars came three vehicles trailed by a dense dust cloud. They came to a halt and some fighter robots of the Arkonide type got out of the cars.

33

Reinforcements, thought Harras, relieved yet with alarm. Like the rest of the soldiers he had in the meantime gotten used to regarding these perfect machine-men as allies and friends. They were united in their task to provide protection for the New Power and to ward off any potential attackers.

Now Lieutenant Becker did something totally incomprehensible: he ordered his men to destroy the robots. The vehicles with the mounted neutroncannons formed a semi-circle in whose focus the robots were standing.

Harras could not manage to draw his hand weapon. He realized that Becker had issued a completely irrational command but didn't have the strength to oppose him. He remained passive and that was all he could do. Out of the corner of his eyes he could see that several of the soldiers seemed to share his feelings. They hesitated to carry out Becker's command.

But that's outright mutiny, thought Harras horrified. Mutiny against Perry Rhodan and the Arkonides. Mutiny against the almighty robot army.

The first cannon spat out a ray of concentrated energy against the unsuspecting robots and thus opened the senseless battle. Four out of a total of nine robot fighters sank half-molten into the broiling desert sand and lay there unmoving. The other five reacted with lightning speed, for machines equipped with positronic thought processes have no reaction lag due to fright like mere human beings.

They were being attacked and it didn't matter by whom. Their left arms rose from their sides and assumed a horizontal position. From inside the robots came a slight clicking sound from a relay, clearing an emergency switch which gave them permission to fire on human beings. Their left arms had thus been transformed into formidable miniature ray cannons.

34

Before Becker's cannons could fire the second round they were hit by the energy showers of the firing robots. Two barrels of Becker's cannons began to droop as if they had turned into soft wax, while a third cannon melted entirely in a shower of sparks.

The rest of Becker's cannons were outside the destruction range. Despite their fast reaction the robots nevertheless had no chance. They were annihilated before they could even whirl around.

Lieutenant Becker drew his own raygun and walked over to the three waiting cars. The three drivers awaited him with faces devoid of any expression. They made no attempt to come to the assistance of their robots.

'You are now under my command!' snapped Becker. The three drivers came to attention, while sitting behind their wheels; they saluted like *one* man.

Sergeant Harras was standing in the background. He hadn't understood what was going on there but he realized that something terrible was taking place in front of his eyes. Becker must suddenly have lost his mind. But – how about himself? Why did he obey these obviously senseless orders? What forced him to do so?

This agonizing headache! It didn't stop. Maybe it was because of the unbearable heat? The sun was standing almost vertically above their heads, sending streams of fire down onto the desert. The nearby hangars and assembly halls were wavering in the heated air.

And then it was as if gentle fingers were groping for his brain and probing around in it. All of a sudden the invisible fingers were no longer gentle but demanding and commanding. They swept aside his will and suspended his normal thought processes.

Like the rest of his group he started to move again, past the still figures of the robots lying on the sand and the disabled, battered, armored tanks.

35

Over at the spaceship docks and hangars he noticed a commotion. Heavily armed men were streaming forth from their pill-boxes. A turbo-car came racing from the right and stopped in front of a building. One of the men carried something in his hand, a small oblong box.

Lieutenant Becker raised his arm. 'Extend your lines! We're attacking the spaceship docks!'

Automatically Sergeant Harras drew his weapon.

*   *   *

Perry Rhodan looked up as someone pushed open the door and rushed into his room. It was his friend Reginald Bell but he could hardly recognize him. He had never before seen him in such a state. His hair was disheveled and his usual ruddy color had given way to a deadly pallor.

His eyes were flashing restlessly and Rhodan was amazed to see his friend's hands tremble.

'Did you run into the devil?' Rhodan asked astonished.

'He'll soon be here,' countered Bell, trying to catch his breath. 'All hell has broken loose. Two guard platoons under Lieutenant Becker's command are attacking our spaceship installations!'

'What did you say?' Rhodan couldn't believe his ears and was beginning to doubt Bell's sanity. 'Becker is attacking the docks? If that's your idea of a joke you've gone too far this time, Reg!'

'No, Perry, it's true! People have gone stark staring mad! I'm sure this is another example of that unknown supermutant's work.'

'The mutant master?' murmured Rhodan, slowly rising from his seat. 'What's going on? What exactly has happened?'

'Just a few seconds ago I got the alarm signal from sector seven. Becker and his men are advancing toward our docks and have already destroyed nine fighter robots. Our defense posts have been alerted and are ready for action. They are awaiting further orders. What are they to do in case Becker actually attacks? That guy has gone crazy!'

Rhodan had a sudden vision of the dying mulatto, who had willed himself to death while obeying the command of the mighty unknown mutant master. If this supermutant was capable of accomplishing this then it wouldn't be surprising if he'd order an entire company to commit suicide.

Fear surged through him. He suddenly realized what might happen if this menacing mutant actually possessed such unbelievable powers. Compared to this the extrasensory abilities of his own mutant corps must seem some ineffective trifling nuisance. Rhodan was overcome by the sudden realization that here he was facing an equally strong, if not superior enemy, who could annihilate him if he was clever enough.

'We can't waste any time now,' Bell urged. 'The men are waiting for our instructions. It won't be easy for them to shoot at their own friends, even if they *have* suddenly gone crazy.'

'We'll go there ourselves,' Rhodan decided. 'Get a psycho raygun and a small gravity neutralizer. Hurry up. I'll wait for you outside in my car.'

Bell whirled around without a word and got cracking. Two minutes later, when Rhodan reached his car, Bell was already there waiting for him. In his left hand he held a small metal box, which did not seem to be too heavy. He clasped a silvery rod in is right hand.

'Is anybody else coming along with us?' asked Bell.

'If we can't manage on our own nobody else can help us,' said Rhodan as he climbed into the car. The turbo-engine started up with a roar and the little machine sped off with unbelievable acceleration, over the smooth expanse of reinforced concrete and in the direction of the docks, just three miles away from the centrally located administrative buildings of Terrania.

There wasn't too much traffic there at this time; occasionally a lone pedestrian stopped and shook his head in bewilderment at this driver gone mad.

Bell gasped for air. 'Can you explain what happened?'

'Hypnotism, what else? The mutant master has placed Becker and his company under his hypnotic influence. We must try and nullify this hypnotic command with our psychobeamer.'

The psychray was an Arkonide weapon. With its help it was possible to take over and direct another person's will and to issue post-hypnotic commands. It had been quite awhile since Rhodan had last found it necessary to resort to its use.

'But how about us?' wondered Bell. 'How come we haven't succumbed to his hypnotic influence? Can't he force his will on us?'

'We know that he tried it once already with Khrest and it didn't work. Therefore I assume that his powers are ineffective when applied to Arkonide brains. Since we have gone through the Arkonide hypno-training, I suppose our brains are now similar in this respect to those of the genuine Arkonides. At least, let's hope so.'

'I hope you're right there, Perry,' remarked Bell and took a deep breath.

They were now racing through the desert. The concrete pavement of the road was 30 feet wide and as smooth as a mirror. The shimmering air hung above the roadway with constantly rippling waves. Ahead they could make out the spaceship installations, the assembly halls and hangars where daily new spaceships of the type of the destroyers were constructed. Rhodan could see indistinct figures running back and forth; big gates were shut and some armored tanks took up positions.

Over to their left in the desert they observed a dust cloud. Underneath that cloud marched Becker with his company of soldiers.

Rhodan couldn't quite explain why the unknown foe of the New Power didn't deploy his forces in another action which would promise a greater likelihood of success. If the supermutant had it in his power to bring entire companies under his influence why then didn't he simply order the New Power pilots to take off with their ships and attack Terrania from the air? Why did he content himself with a relatively harmless fighting action whose success was a priori, to say the least, doubtful? It made no sense.

Did the unknown supermutant intend to make Rhodan a nervous wreck?

Well, apparently he had already succeeded with Bell. The Minister of Security of the New Power had meanwhile become a model of fear and trepidation. If John Marshall had been present he would certainly have now called him the Minister of Insecurity. Bell kept fidgeting with the psycho ray and was wiggling restlessly in his seat.

'Oh, stop wiggling like a worm, Reggie!' Rhodan admonished him. 'You can be sure that the supermutant won't be satisfied with this attempt. It's just a beginning.'

'A beginning?' moaned Bell in horror. 'Our own people shooting at us and you call that just a beginning?'

Rhodan didn't answer. He knew his friend sufficiently well to realize that his loss of composure was but skin deep.

The car now passed the first robot guard outposts.

Several pulse-ray cannons were mounted, ready for action.

They drove up to a bunker. Some officers were standing about. They wore the uniforms of the guard division. They came running toward the car as soon as they recognized its occupants.

Bell didn't give them a chance to say anything. 'Clear the area!' he shouted. He jumped out of the car, waving his psychray. 'I'll show you how one can command an entire army!'

Rhodan took the small metal box away from Bell and placed it on the ground before him. He seemed suddenly not to be overconfident as to how well the hypnotizing silver rod would work in this situation. He signaled to Bell: 'Give it a try! Order them to make an about face and to return immediately to their quarters.' Them Rhodan addressed the waiting officers. 'Now you, gentlemen, keep your men in readiness. But don't give any orders to shoot unless I specifically tell you so. We don't want to have to kill our own people.'

'But they've destroyed nine robots already,' said a captain.

'That's most regrettable but robots aren't human beings. Besides, Becker and his men were acting against their own free will.'

'Against their will?' echoed the captain with a questioning voice. But before he could ask any further questions, his attention was diverted. For now Bell had gone into action.

The psychobeam's range was naturally limited but meanwhile Lieutenant Becker's forces had approached close enough. It was an absolute mystery why he took up position close by. He could have opened fire on the docks from a distance of over a mile away. His cannons were powerful enough over such a distance. Instead he advanced to half a mile within the lines of the boarder guard sentinels.

Bell kneeled on the ground and pointed his silvery rod at the involuntary opponent. Then he depressed the activating knob. At the same time he spoke loud and clear: 'Lieutenant Becker, I'm ordering you and your men to turn around and march back at once to your quarters. All other orders you might have received are herewith countermanded.'

The officers – their number had increased to five meanwhile – stared at Bell with admiring eyes. They knew the Arkonides were said to possess legendary weapons but they had never before seen any of them in action. At least not the psychray. Unfortunately however they were not destined to witness this miracle today either.

For Lieutenant Becker paid not the slightest heed to Bell's commands.

The first shot swept close above the heads of the little group and its impact and heat reduced to one clump of molten metal a guard robot who had unconcernedly been making his rounds a few yards further back.

'The supermutant's power is greater than that of our psycho-ray,' remarked Rhodan calmly. He had in the meantime completed his preparations and was squatting, ready for action, beside the rim of the sheltered concrete dug out. At any moment he could quickly duck into this shelter, if he would deem it necessary. The five officers had already taken cover in the bunker. They had radioed to their men who were dispersed in the area to await further orders and under no circumstances to open fire on the mutineers.

Bell tried his luck again. He directed the hypo-beam once more at Becker's men, issued a second command which was ignored just like the first. The situation grew critical. For now three neutron cannons blasted away at the nearest spaceship assembly halls.

It was then that Rhodan realized that he would be unable to defeat the supermutant's hypnotic powers with mental weapons. Only brute force could overcome his influence on Becker's group. Rhodan pointed the objective of the gravity neutralizor toward the mutineers. He released the activating switch.

The effective range of the instrument was fanshaped, beginning directly in front of it and spreading out in the direction of the opponent, its efficiency diminishing with distance. Its efficacy however was still sufficient to render Becker, his men and all their equipment weightless.

Sergeant Harras was just putting one foot in front of the other, most unwillingly since he saw no valid reason for doing so, when suddenly he became detached from the ground. He was gently floating upward while slowly spinning like a top. Fear-struck, he let go of his weapon but it did not drop to the ground, rather it remained constantly at the same height as himself.

Harras' fate was shared by all the others of his group. Lieutenant Becker, who leapt across to one of the canons, was hardest hit by the sudden loss of gravity. Like a human missile he shot diagonally up into the clear desert sky, flailing his arms and legs desperately trying in vain to grab ahold of something in the empty air. Unfortunately, Rhodan was unable to continue observing his flight. The unlucky lieutenant passed shortly beyond the effective range of the neutralizor and plummeted like a stone to the ground. He was the sole victim of the attack that had been forced upon him, apart from the three drivers and three gunners riding in the armored tanks which had been destroyed earlier by the robots.

Almost the entire fighting forces under Lieutenant Becker's command were now hovering high up in the air. They assumed various positions depending on the respective movements with which they had become detached from the ground when they were rendered weightless. Since however the Arkonide instrument's range was not unlimited it was imperative to act now in order to prevent any additional accidents and fatalities.

Rhodan turned to the officers who had followed the entire procedure utterly dumbfounded and delighted. 'I'm now diminishing the intensity of the neutralizor. Send your men out to capture the airborne company as they will be landing again on firm ground. Have your men move with extreme caution across the terrain – it's subject to only one-tenth normal gravity. Watch out for Becker's fighting tanks as they come down. If necessary you'll have to render their gunners harmless.'

It was amazing how fast the officers recovered from their state of perplexity. It took hardly a few minutes for them to mobilize their soldiers, who then proceeded to very slowly advance with peculiar, slinking steps toward the slowly sinking figures who helplessly were fidgeting in the air, struck with horror. Most had simply released their grip on their weapons and thus no longer presented any danger.

Gradually Rhodan reinstated normal conditions of gravity and then waited until the mutineering company had been subdued. He had meanwhile taken the beamer from Bell's hand and screened the soldiers against any further hypnotic commands emanating from the master enemy mutant. He sensed instinctively that such a screening-off was entirely possible while the Arkonide instrument was ineffective to pierce through a hypnotic block once it had been placed in a victim.

Hardly five minutes passed and the supermutant withdrew.

Sergeant Harras felt all of a sudden how the pressure in his head was getting weaker and finally leaving him completely. At first he couldn't understand where he was, he thought he was still lying at the bottom of the swiming pool and was most startled to peer suddenly into the threatening orifices of guns pointed at him. Rhodan in person explained what had happened to Harras and his comrades. He also pointed out to them that this mysterious incident might repeat itself at any time. Since however they didn't expect any armed attack from the outside, the weapons in the hands of the guards were to be reduced to a bare minimum.

Not far from them, off to one side, lay the motionless figure of Lieutenant Becker. Bell threw a glance in that direction and with a somber face, murmured: 'That's the ninth victim already today, Perry. It's time to undertake some decisive action.'

Rhodan did not reply. Silently they drove back to Terrania, where some more bad news awaited them. Major Freyt had received a messaged from New York where the financial genius of the New Power, Homer G. Adams, had his headquarters. From there the mutant with the eidetic memory extended his network of influence, ruling the economies of the whole world. Homer seemed to be infallible and had never made a wrong decision. At least not as long as there hadn't been the supermutant. The first attacks of the unknown enemy had been warded off without irreparable damage but Perry Rhodan had taken preventive measures and had sent little Betty Toufry to protect his financial genius. Betty was the most powerful telepath *and* telekineticist in Rhodan's mutant corps.

And the alarming report had been sent by her.

As earlier, Homer G. Adams seemed to have become affected by the mutant master's sinister influence. Homer's latest financial deals obviously lacked common-sense and would have been disastrous for the General Cosmic Company.

At the last minute Betty succeeded in cancelling his business dispositions by applying her psychobeamer. As long as she remained in Adams' presence he was safe from outside hypnotic influences but she could not accompany him day and night wherever he went.

Rhodan at once established communication with the General Cosmic Company. The picture of an embarrassed Homer G. Adams came onto the screen. He was a rather short man, his thin hair for ever looking disheveled, and now he made the impression of having spent a few nights without sleep. Betty Toufry sat in the background. She too looked extremely tired.

'Hello, Adams,' began Perry Rhodan as if New York were only a few miles distant and not halfway around the world. 'I was told you've experienced some difficulties again.' Adams attempted to answer but Rhodan did not wish to be interrupted. 'You needn't apologize, Mr. Adams. We've lately been through similar trouble here ourselves. The power of our opponent extends over the whole globe. There's one thing I'd like to know from you. Could you tell when the influence begins to make itself felt?'

Adams slowly nodded his head. 'Yes, I first notice a pressure in my head but by then it is already too late. If little Betty hadn't been near me I really don't know what would have happened. I'm very sorry about this but I don't think you can count on me from now on. I'm no longer a reliable help to you.'

'Nonsense, Adams, don't say that. Remain passive until you receive further instructions from me. Avoid any important business deals in the next few days. And the moment the enemy exposes himself in the slightest way – and I believe this is inevitable – we'll be ready to strike.'

'I hope this'll happen soon. I assure you it's most unpleasant to be constantly threatened with loss of control of your five senses.'

Rhodan smiled at him reassuringly and cut off the connection.

But the moment Adams' image had disappeared from the screen, Rhodan's smile also vanished.

* * *

There was nothing extraordinary in Fellmer Lloyd's appearance, he looked like the typical man next door. Many years ago he had worked in an atomic power station as assistant to the chief scientist. But then he had been tracked down and discovered by Rhodan's agents.

For Fellmer Lloyd was a natural mutant.

He could not accurately be described as a genuine telepath but his abilities closely resembled those of the true mind readers. A part of his brain had undergone changes due to the radiation his parents had been exposed to. As a consequence he was at any time in a position to absorb the brain-wave patterns of other people around him, sort them out and analyze them. He couldn't read their thoughts but he could recognize their basic emotions and consequently more or less judge their intentions. When talking to another person he knew at once if he was friend or enemy. He used this talent by working as a 'spotter' for the mutant corps.

Fellmer Lloyd was standing inconspicuously near the exit barrier of the Moscow airport, scanning attentively the departing and arriving passengers of the regularly scheduled jet plane. This plane was one of the passenger crafts that daily commuted between the New Power and the various continents of the world. This airline was sponsored by the New Power.

Only last week two of these machines had been destroyed in midair by an act of sabotage. The Ministry of Security of the New Power had therefore deployed some

46

mutants in order to prevent a recurrence of such incidents.

Fellmer Lloyd was one of the mutants who had been charged with this mission. He was flying from continent to continent, cautiously probing all the passengers' brain-wave pattern, endeavoring to make sure that no saboteur would slip aboard.

He hadn't yet made up his mind whether he should leave again the capital city of the Eastern Bloc on this particular flight. He like Moscow; he had made friends here. Everybody seemed so pleasant and kind that he didn't like the idea of departing so soon.

Only superficially he checked out the elegant couple that was just passing through the barrier and then proceeded to cross the asphalt strip leading to the jet plane. Probably some newly-weds starting out on their honeymoon. Harmless, in any case, he quickly stated.

In the background he saw the roofs of the city, glittering in the light of the setting sun. Towering sky-scrapers reared up into the clear sky, trying to gather the last rays of the sinking sun. The broad freeway leading from the city to the airport was brightly illuminated. There was dense traffic.

Fellmer Lloyd suddenly was startled out of his contemplation of that peaceful evening scene. From somewhere surged something evil. Somebody was thinking of violence and caution, murder and death.

The range of his mind-searching ability was not very extensive, only a few hundred yards. But judging by the intensity of the brain-waves that were overwhelming him, they must originate in his immediate vicinity.

Hastily he looked around.

People were standing in little groups all about. They were talking to each other, saying goodby, embracing and waving a last greeting. A young lady with unusually pretty legs was striding with determined steps across the barrier and the waiting machine. She carried a large brown leather bag in her hand. Over to the left, Fellmer Lloyd noticed a policeman who attentively was scanning the crowd.

Lloyd's glance returned to the young lady. His brain was now registering stronger impressions. Yes, indeed, these violent thoughts emanated from her; no doubt. For a moment the mutant believed he had been mistaken but he knew he could trust his sense of orientation.

Cautiously he set himself in motion, walking behind the young lady. She was wearing a modern suit and gave the impression of being the sports type. Her gait was elastic, almost soft.

Three minutes before take-off.

He walked up the gangway and saw how the young lady presented her ticket and the number of her seat to the stewardess. Then she went inside the plane. Lloyd followed her. He showed his identity card to the stewardess; that was enough to let him aboard. The stewardess assigned him the seat diagonally across from the young lady.

The thoughts of something horrible became weaker now and finally gave way to a sense of security. Lloyd knew then for sure that there was no threat of immediate danger. But he also knew that he mustn't let this pretty young lady out of his sight, not even for a moment, during the entire flight.

She seemed to be about 25 years old, was slender and had dark brown hair. Her somewhat narrow eyes lent her oval face a special charm and Lloyd had trouble realizing that she could be an agent of the unknown supermutant. Perhaps all of this was nothing but a mere coincidence.

The plane took off, pursuing the setting sun. They flew

at such speed that the sun was still standing at the same height in the horizon when they landed at the airport at Berlin-Tempelhof.

Lloyd was suddenly flooded by a wave of excitement coming from the young girl as she rose from her seat and walked to the exit door of the plane. The plane had stopped close to the big customs shed.

Fellmer got up and tried not to let his victim out of his sight. Her brain-wave pattern had become so intensified that Fellmer felt it almost unbearable. Painfully these patterns surged into his awareness and aroused in him the urgent sensation of imminent danger.

She had walked down the gangway and was now hurrying toward the barrier. She held her ticket in her hand. Apparently she had no hand luggage.

No hand luggage?

Lloyd felt for a moment as if somebody had poured a bucket full of boiling water over his back. Luggage?

He realized now what had happened. The young lady carried no luggage therefore she must have left her brown leather bag on the plane.

Lloyd abruptly made an about-face and ran back to the plane. He pushed his way through the exiting passengers, paying no attention to their infuriated protesting voices, and raced to the place where the suspect had been sitting.

Her leather bag was still underneath her seat.

He picked it up with one swoop and raced back to the exit. He looked around, trying to locate her, afraid that he might have lost her. He ran out of the building and saw the owner of the bag just trying to hail a taxi. Lloyd monitored again her confused thought pattern, into which now again feelings of insecurity had crept. Should she not really be convinced that what she had been doing was really the right thing?

Bounding forward he arrived at the taxi just in time, flung open the door and jumped in. He peered directly into the wide open, horrified eyes of the young girl, that were not at all interested in the intruder but only in the leather bag he was holding in his hand.

'Young lady,' began Lloyd, groaning with exhaustion, 'are you in a hurry! You forgot your bag on the plane.'

She examined his face with a searching glance, then fear flitted across her features. She quickly reached into her suit pocket and pulled out a snub-nosed revolver. But Lloyd had already been alerted by a corresponding brain-wave pattern change from the young lady. He quickly disarmed her.

'But my dear young lady,' he warned gently. 'I have only your best interests at heart . . .'

'You are lying.' She shook her head. She spoke English with a strong Russian accent. 'You've been following me ever since Moscow. Do you really believe I didn't notice?'

'You can read minds?'

She hesitated for a moment then replied: 'Yes, I'm a telepath.'

For an instant Lloyd was disappointed and even frightened. How should he handle a person who could guess even his innermost thoughts? But then he shrugged his shoulders.

'Alright, then we needn't pretend. Let's be frank with each other. You were under orders from the super-mutant to sabotage the airlines of the New Power. There's a time bomb ticking away in your leather bag. You set the mechanism and left the bomb on the plane. Between Berlin and London the bomb would have exploded. Did I guess right?'

She looked him up and down with a scornful glance. 'So what?'

50

'In this case Perry Rhodan would be most interested to have a talk with you.'

A shadow flitted across her pretty face. 'I'm not in the least interested in having a talk with a traitor of all mankind. You can tell him that from me. By the way, if I were you I'd take care to get rid of that bag over there. It contains explosives powerful enough to send the two of us sky high. I'm the only one who knows when it is set to go off.'

'As long as you are with me and don't show any signs of apprehension, I know nothing will happen,' countered Lloyd with satisfied logic. He leaned forward and pushed aside the glass partition. 'Driver, take us back to the airport.' He closed the glass partition and turned to his prisoner. 'It's time we got to know each other. Since you already are familiar with my name, of course, may I ask what yours is?'

'Tatjana Michalowna,' she answered in a defiant tone. He sensed clearly that she wasn't lying. 'But that's all you'll find out from me.'

'Believe me, that won't work with Perry Rhodan and his mutants,' he assured her, smiling sarcastically. He was satisfied to note that she now seemed frightened. 'I've a fast jet waiting at the airport. We'll be in Terrania in a short while.'

She remained silent. Her eyes were resting thoughtfully on her brown leather bag, which sat on the floor next to Lloyd. He noticed her glance and smiled. 'Don't worry, my dear. Somewhere in Siberia that explosion won't harm anybody. Years ago they were used to much bigger ones than that thing you brought.'

Stubbornly, she still didn't utter a word.

*　　　*　　　*

The mental duel between John Marshall and Tatjana

Michalowna lasted only a short time. Then the Russian girl knew that it made no sense for her to continue lying. In addition to that there was another factor she had not counted on: Perry Rhodan.

With a halting voice she began to speak. 'Like the majority of mankind I was skeptical toward the New Power. For me you were a traitor, Mr. Rhodan, for you entered into an alliance with extraterrestrial life forms and strove to rule the whole world. I admit you prevented the atom war between the East and the West but this didn't entitle you to force a development on us which is progressing too fast and throws us out of our prescribed path. We would have managed very well without you in our goal of uniting this world.'

'I'm convinced of that,' retorted Rhodan with a mischievous smile, 'but you'd have done the uniting in your own way. I preferred mine. Any objections?'

'Certainly. In any case, one day I met a man in whose mind I could detect an agreement with my own thoughts regarding you. He too condemned the New Power and desired peace. *Our* peace. I got in touch with him and since he had no idea of my telepathic gifts I found out everything. Another power has come into being, a purely human power, which has nothing to do with the Arkonides or any other galactic races. The mutant master's policy is concerned exclusively with Earthly affairs and not galactic interests.'

'Very narrowminded,' said Rhodan. 'But, please, go on.'

'I joined the supermutant and his forces,' she continued. 'His fight is just, for it is directed against something that is alien to human nature and will forever remain so.'

'That same xenophobia was once typical of all the small European nations who used to believe that the culture of their neighboring countries was inferior and that therefore they could never be united and live in peace with each other,' interjected Perry Rhodan. 'And today they *are united*!'

'This was a natural process, no artificial union ...'

'Don't say that. They were helped along on that path.'

'Nevertheless ...'

'There is no difference. Mankind had to learn that it is not the only intelligent life in the universe. Should mankind remain in isolation in order to one day become the victim of a hostile invader's surprise attack? Or isn't it better to adjust to your surroundings? That's all we are really doing! Only a united Earth, with a strong leadership, will not fail to join up with the rest of the galactic civilizations – *on a par* with them. Not too long ago, such developments seemed to lie in the very remote future for mankind; they were looked upon like the wild dreams fantasy writers. But today it has become reality. We must make the decision – and many have done so already. There's nothing even a supermutant can do about that.'

'He doesn't intend to but he is against you as the sole ruler.'

Rhodan smiled and quickly glanced at Marshall. 'If I had wanted to be the sole ruler of mankind I could have done so a long time ago. You surely must admit that.'

She was hesitant. 'It's true. Why didn't you do it, then?'

'Because it didn't matter to me. Peace-loving people should see to it that there is order but they should never attempt to rule and force their will on others.'

'Do you consider yourself the policing force of this globe, or even the peacelord of the universe?'

'In a way. But we are mainly trying to pave the way for a better understanding among the nations of this

Earth and a peaceful co-existence with the rest of intelligent life all over the universe.

She did not answer but it was obvious that she was pondering what she had just heard. John Marshall the telepath said suddenly: 'How come I can't always receive your thoughts? I've never before encountered anyone who could conceal their thoughts from me.'

'Well, you've met one now,' smiled Tatjana superciliously. 'Besides being a telepath I've another talent which is not as generally well-known as I used to assume. I can erect a shield against any strange influence; maybe this causes at the same time my thoughts to be screened off so that not even another esper can penetrate through this barrier.'

'Are you capable of protecting yourself against foreign influences?' asked Rhodan with great interest. 'Do you find this necessary? There are only very few people who are hypnos.'

'The mutant master is a hypno,' said Tatjana emphatically.

Rhodan had a good long look at her before he continued. 'And you are able to ward off his remote hypnotic control over you?'

He waited until the girl had nodded in agreement. Then he said: 'This means you can at this instant act against his will?' She nodded once more to confirm what he surmised to be true. 'Do you realize that he issues orders to his collaborators to will themselves to death as soon as they fall into our hands?'

She grew pale. 'And?' she asked terrified.

'They actually obey his command and die,' said Rhodan with brutal candor. 'So you be very careful to maintain this shield. You are probably the only living human being over which the supermutant has no control. Except for us, of course, because he doesn't know our brain-

54

wave patterns. He can exert a certain influence but can't give orders to our hearts to stop.'

'That's horrible!' she exclaimed. Tatjana could not get over the fact that her master was a person without scruples. Rhodan took advantage of this situation.

'The mutant master caused one of my companies to mutineer and forced them to shoot at their own comrades. Fortunately we could prevent him from completely carrying out his evil plans.'

Tatjana clapped her hands over her face. 'And I was so deluded that I almost murdered hundreds of innocent people. The bomb ...'

'Don't think back on that,' Rhodan said softly and with emphasis. 'Many men have done worse things acting in good faith. You followed your own convictions. As soon as you've recovered from this unpleasant experience, Lloyd will return you to Moscow. Nobody forces you to stay here.'

She regarded him in amazement. 'You'll let me go free?'

'Why should I hold you against your will? I hardly believe you'll ever again make the same mistake of letting yourself be misled by stupid slogans. The super-mutant is not merely a narrowminded zealot, he's also a criminal thirsting for power. Some day I'll learn who hides beneath the mask of the mutant master.'

Tatjana raised her head and her eyes were filled with surprise as she looked straight into Rhodan's eyes. 'You don't know who he is?' she asked.

Rhodan shook his head but his steel-gray eyes became suddenly cold and more alert than usual. 'Do you?' he asked.

Tatjana seemed to savor the moment when she could feel superior to a giant like Perry Rhodan. She nodded and replied: 'I even have met him in person.'

3 WORLD ENEMY #1

In the vicinity of Alamogordo, where the first atom bomb was detonated in 1945, a nuclear reactor accident occurred during testing. Many scientists and workers were killed by the leaking radiation but just as many people who worked there escaped with their lives.

Among these was the physicist Monterny, who married a short time afterwards. His marriage was very brief but also very happy. His wife bore him a son, Clifford Monterny. Clifford was a mutant of the first degree, a hypno of incredible power.

Like his father before him, Clifford studied physics. Due to his superior intelligence he obtained an influential position and acquired a considerable fortune but he was no longer a youngster when he discovered his unusual mutant characteristics. He could force his will on others with the greatest of ease. It took him two years to find out that this hypnotic influence was not restricted by spatial distances. Once he had met, or even only seen a person, he could locate and influence them with his extrasensory powers.

Clifford Monterny was fat, puffy and unattractive. Women shunned him, which certainly had an effect on the development of his character. His small, deepset eyes always bore an expression of distrust and envy. At the age of 32 he had already lost all his hair, a fact he tried to hide by usually wearing a hat. His outstanding intelligence stood in harsh contrast to his disagreeable exterior.

With great interest he followed the founding of the

New Power and the successful path taken by Perry Rhodan. He observed how Rhodan's mutant corps was organized and more than once he was tempted to put his talents at Rhodan's disposal. But he never took the decisive step.

After all, wasn't he a superior mutant in his own right? If he so chose, couldn't he himself guide the destiny of mankind? Was he not capable of concentrating more power in his hands than ever anybody alive before him? Why not set up a mutant corps of his own?

And thus Clifford Monterny began to gather, in all secrecy, a group of mutants around him.

Clifford Monterny became the master of the mutants, a man known hardly to anyone but one who seemed to be everywhere – and nowhere. Thanks to his considerable fortune he built a veritable fortress in the mountains of Utah. Nearly 60 miles to the east of the great Salt Lake, at the foot of Emmons Peak, was his farm and adjoining land covering an area of nearly four square miles. His house resembled a fortress which had been made impregnable. All the latest modern technical devices had been installed to insure proper announcement of any visitors and their surveillance. Any unwelcome visitors or intruders would of course be effectively repelled.

When Clifford Monterny reached the age of 35 his telepathic abilities had finally matured and reached their peak. Combined with his hypno talent he was now able to dominate unconditionally any person he had once encountered and whose vibration pattern was known to him. There was no escape for his unfortunate victims for he would infallibly find them again wherever they might try to flee.

Shrouded in complete secrecy, the headquarters of a malign power had grown in the rocky mountains of Utah, an organization that threatened even Perry Rhodan's existence. Their first attack on the financial and economic strength of the New Power had been warded off by Perry Rhodan but now the mutant master was concentrating on more direct methods of striking at the heart of the realm of the Power.

At this point in the development of this struggle Perry Rhodan finally found out the identity of his unknown, bitter foe.

*　　　*　　　*

All the secret services of the world had joined in one organization, the Terranian Defense Federation. The General Secretary of this influential federation was Allan D. Mercant.

Mercant was hastily running his fingers through the thin crown of blond hair, trying to pat the unruly strands into place, when a visitor was announced.

'Rhodan in person?' he asked to reassure himself. It had been ages since he had last talked to him. 'What are you standing around for? Hurry up and show him in!'

The young officer whirled around so swiftly that he almost knocked over Rhodan who entered the room smilingly cordially in greeting to Mercant. 'It's good to see you again. You still look as lively as ever.'

'Don't be deceived by my looks, I'm getting on in age,' complained Mercant bitterly and smoothed the wispy curls on his temples. His temples had turned gray but the blond of his thin wreath of hair around his big skull had stubbornly retained its color, thought Rhodan with a sudden suspicion. 'To what do I owe the honor of your visit?'

'Nothing pleasant brings me here,' replied Rhodan and sat down on the proferred chair. 'I need your help.'

'Help?' Marcant's eyes looked saucer-like in astonishment. 'I am supposed to help *you*?'

'This time, yes,' smiled Rhodan; 'it's an exception; I don't want to cause any political difficulties. You know yourself how sensitive some people's feelings are in that respect.'

'How true,' nodded Mercant to express his agreement and compassion. 'After all, we still don't have a United Government of the World.'

Rhodan leaned forward and looked inquiringly into Mercant's eyes. 'Do you know a Clifford Monterny?'

Mercant's face grew pensive and he reflected for awhile, then hesitantly he nodded his head. 'I know of him but haven't met him personally.'

'Very fortunate for you,' interjected Rhodan. Mercant overlooked this remark.

'There was once a well-known physicist by the name of Monterny but he lost his life quite some time ago during an explosion.'

'That was the father. I mean his son Clifford.'

'Isn't he a physicist, too? Yes, I know of him. He's made a few inventions but has never come to the attention of the Terranian Defense Federation. Seems to have a lot of money. Has a ranch somewhere out west. But what do you want to know that for?'

'I'd like to obtain your permission to fly over the territory of the United States with a squadron of my space-destroyers and raze Monterny's ranch to the ground. I hope you understand now why it is necessary for me first to get some official sanction.'

'What do you want? I believe ...' shouted Mercant excitedly.

'Don't believe anything, Mercant. Clifford Monterny is the mysterious mutant master, in case you are interested. He is about to shake the world order to its very foundations. He is a hypno and can cause any statesman of this globe at any moment to drop his country's stockpile of atom bombs over their neighbor's territory. Clifford Monterny is world enemy number one. Only his ruthless extinction can save us all from certain ruin. This is why I came to see you.'

Mercant had already turned to a table mike and spoke into it his request to the FBI to supply him with all available data on Monterny. Then he looked up. 'You can count on my complete cooperation, Rhodan. Within a few minutes we should be in touch with the President of the USA. But one question in the mean time: where are your destroyers now?'

Rhodan smiled gently. 'Overhead, my dear Mercant. Exactly 18 miles above us. Are you surprised?'

*   *   *

Cadet Tifflor saw in front of him the rounded disk of Terra. It was surrounded by a milky layer of the denser atmosphere, then the sky's color gradually deepened from violet to black. The bigger stars were shimmering without sparkling, although the sun was shining.

Without special formalities Tiff had been transferred by Perry Rhodan to the fleet of the New Power. He had been entrusted with the command of a destroyer. Together with Ray Gall and Pete Maros he was positioned now with his Z-35 at a height of 18 miles above the headquarters of the Terranian Defense Federation, where Perry Rhodan was presently negotiating with Mercant.

Eight additional destroyers were hovering close by, supported in place by their gravity neutralizors. Much higher up, invisible to the naked eye, stood the mighty spaceship *Stardust II* in the void of space. Bell acted as the commander replacing Rhodan who was on Earth. The New Power had begun its action against the mutant master.

Mercant had issued the necessary instructions and nobody would attempt to bother the nine cruisers that were waiting above the territory of the United States. Besides, there was no weapon against the mighty spacesphere of the *Stardust II*, whose diameter was almost half a mile.

Tiff breathed a sigh of relief when the screen before him lit up showing the familiar face of Reginald Bell. Tiff knew that all the commanders of the other eight destroyers were simultaneously put in touch with the *Stardust II*.

'Calling all destroyers! Rhodan will arrive in a few minutes here on the *Stardust II* via an auxiliary vessel. Action will proceed according to plan. Adhere to permanent instructions!'

The picture screen remained brightly lit. Bell's face moved sideways and out of view. The audio contact was interrupted. This lasted 10 minutes, then came data on which course the destroyers were to set. Bell's calm voice guided the nine destroyers to their destination.

*   *   *

Deep down below the Earth's surface lay Clifford Monterny's command center.

Surrounded by innumerable picture screens and other communication devices sat the supermutant in his command center like a spider in its gigantic web. He held in his hands all the strings of his far flung enterprise and from here the monster was directing his battles which were mainly conducted in an inconspicuous manner.

One of the screens lit up. The face of an Oriental man came on. The image was flickering and distorted. There must be many relay stations between the sender and the receiver of this broadcast.

'What do you have to report, S-7?' asked Monterny.

'While conducting new research experiments the Syntak Works were destroyed last night. They are in Australia and 65 % of its stock is owned by the General Cosmic Company.'

'Thank you, S-7, you'll get your check.'

The screen grew dark. Another face came on as another screen shone brightly. A black man. 'This is M-3 speaking. This morning the Governor of Sirapolis died during a traffic accident. The driver of the car escaped unknown.'

'Good, M-3. You know your next mission?'

'I received instructions from ...'

'That'll do, M-3. I'm awaiting your report: mission accomplished.'

A third screen. 'Hello, chief. This is Sp-6. Unusual flight activity observed in the air space above the Terranian Defense Federation. Sighted a spacesphere. The FBI was requested to provide data regarding Clifford Monterny.'

'What did you say?' Monterny leaned forward. 'About me?'

'I have this information from an absolutely reliable source. chief. The only thing I couldn't find out is who asked for this information.'

'Dammit, that's impossible. Nobody knows my identity. Or should perhaps ...?'

He had a sudden vision of the oval face of a pretty woman with whom he had lost contact for a few days.

Tatjana Michalowna!

He had lost touch with her when she failed to execute her last mission. He knew that she was a powerful telepath, just like himself. But in addition she had the special gift of being able to place a protective screen around her brain and thus elude outside influences. Even his own.

Could Tatjana have dared betray him? And why? Hadn't she been one of his most loyal and most firmly convinced followers? He had always had to be on his guard when she was around not to think any 'wrong thoughts.'

'It must have been one of our own people,' Monterny heard his agent's reply. 'As soon as I find out who demanded these data about you from the FBI I'll report again to you.' Monterny paused for a minute with the reception of his agents' newscast. He was deeply absorbed in his thoughts. His superbrain reached out and searched where his mutants were in all parts of the world. This was not always an easy task and this was the reason he kept up this daily news report for all routine announcements. But if necessary he could keep his agents under surveillance without technical installations.

He currenly had 13 mutants under his command. One of them, the most important one, could not report, since he was not on Earth. Eleven mutants called in and were instructed to return to the base immediately. One mutant only did not answer Monterny's call: Tatjana Michalowna.

The supermutant did not waste any time with long reflections. He sounded the first-stage alarm. The first of his mutants were due to arrive soon. The entire fortress was put in a state of defense.

Tiny jet planes were now coming in for a landing on the vast fields surrounding the farm house. They were bringing Monterny's main assistants, the mutants. They had left their posts and were rushing back to headquarters in order to receive new and direct orders. In the underground shafts of the former mines a feverish activity unfolded. Modern artillery was carried close below the surface by freight elevators and then placed in strategic positions, ready for action. All was accomplished completely automatically and by electronic guidance.

The mutant master sat in his command center and kept everything under his control. On various screens he could observe the environs of his farm house in all details but hard as he might try he couldn't detect any suspicious movements. There was no sign of any potential attacker.

Perhaps agent Sp-6 had been mistaken and this request from the FBI was just a routine matter; but he couldn't be too careful in his position. If only his man in Terrania would get in touch with him.

Monterny had no idea that this man would never again get in touch with him. As strenuously as his searching mind was trying to locate him, Monterny was unable to find a dead man's brain. Tatjana had taken care that no threat any longer existed for Terrania from this end. When put under arrest this agent was shot in self-defense.

But the supermutant knew nothing of these events. He was waiting in vain for some news from his agent in Terrania. And thus he also remained ignorant of whether Perry Rhodan might have learned something about his identity.

All was quiet for the time being.

But at the slightest sign of an impending attack the harmless Monterny ranch would change into a fire-spewing fortress.

The mutant master had mobilized his defense forces and was all set, ready for action.

*   *   *

Perry Rhodan and Reginald Bell took their time.

The *Stardust II* and the nine destroyers had climbed to the edge of the atmosphere in order to foil all attempts to locate him by the mutant master's radar installations. They were now holding their final council of war.

'Our mutants have done a splended job,' reported Bell

and threw a warning glance in the direction of Pucky, who was squatting in a corner. 'Several agents of the supermutant were put out of action. We couldn't catch any of his mutants. According to Tatjana there were 12 other mutants besides herself. She knows 11 in person but not the 12th. He seems to be an extraordinarily capable specimen.'

'More capable than I?' asked Pucky from his corner.

This was actually very difficult to imagine. As far as his looks were concerned, Pucky would not be surpassed by any human being, for Pucky did not belong to the human race. Some time back, when Rhodan had set out on his search for the Immortal and had made a temporary landing on the lonely planet Vagabond while on his way from the planet Wanderer, the mouse-beaver Pucky, as he was later christened by a member of the crew, had stowed away on board the *Stardust*. From that moment on the little mouse-beaver had been inseparable from Rhodan and Bell. Pucky's fur was reddish-brown; he had the head of a mouse and the tail of a beaver, which he used for additional support when he was walking upright. His extraordinary intelligence had enabled him to learn very quickly the language of the 'two-legged creatures.' He was an outstanding telepath, master to perfection of the art of telekinesis and teleportation. On occasion it had happened that he would cause an entire fleet of smaller spaceships to execute the fanciest maneuvers much against the will of their pilots.

Bell examined the little mouse-beaver quizzically. 'To a certain extent he might perhaps be more capable than you, Pucky, but we don't know that for sure. But please, don't disturb us now, even if you are a full-fledged member of the mutant corps, we must discuss very important matters now.' Bell concluded excitedly and looked at

65

Rhodan. 'Where was I when we were so rudely interrupted?'

'We were talking about Monterny's mutants. They've already been alerted.'

'That't right. Our radarite Tanaka Seiko has intercepted the thought message sent out by the mutant master and also his subsequent telecast. Tanaka located each of the receiving stations and drew a sketch. Here it is.'

Rhodan took the piece of paper and studied the drawing. It reminded him of a spider's web. In the middle, at the focal point, sat the supermutant. Innumerable lines were spreading out from this center in all directions. These lines led to the respective mutants and agents. Rhodan's men were already on their way to each of Monterny's men.

'Excellent,' Rhodan said. 'This will effectively isolate the mutant master. He no longer will be able to count on assistance from the outside.'

'I doubt this will matter greatly to him. Don't forget Tifflor's report. His prisoner was talking about Mars. I'm afraid that Monterny has at some time added another base to his wide-flung network, a base on Mars.'

'Right now he's still sitting here on Earth and that's where we'll get him and finish him off. I've never been so determined to stamp out an opponent utterly.' Rhodan's voice had assumed a steel-like quality. 'The mutant master is the declared enemy of all mankind. He wants to unite all men but under his iron rule. The ultimate world dictator.'

'We'll ruin his plan for him, you can rely on that,' promised Bell and glanced at his watch. 'Our shock troops should have reached Monterny's ranch by now. They should be in the vicinity. I wonder why we didn't get any report from them?'

'They may have run into difficulties. In any case, we won't wait much longer now, we'll start the action very soon. If possible I want our men to take Monterny alive.'

Bell's eyes resembled good-sized saucers. 'Why? In order to imprison him? He'll get away again and then the whole chase will start all over. No, if we catch him, I'm in favor of wiping him out for good.'

'I'm thinking of his mutants,' demurred Rhodan. 'I'm convinced they know just as little about their master's despicable deeds as Tatjana did.'

'But aren't they committing some crimes, even if they obey their master?'

'They are acting under duress, Reggie. They believe they are acting for a good and just cause. Well, we'll soon enough find out for ourselves . . .'

The door to the command center opened. 'A report from Utah,' exclaimed the radioman excitedly. 'They want to talk to you, Mr. Rhodan.'

Bell arrived at the communication center even faster than Perry Rhodan. Pucky waddled behind them at a leisurely pace.

'This is Wuriu Sengu speaking,' came a voice from the loudspeaker after Rhodan had given the password. Sengu was the Jananese 'scout', the seer of the mutant corps. He could see through solid matter and discover any object he wanted to find even behind steel walls. 'I'm not quite two miles from Monterny's farm house. I managed to land and creep toward the house unnoticed. Everything seems quiet inside the house itself. I can't locate a living soul in it. But under the ground there's a lot going on. An unbelievable system of defense installations. Long corridors with branch passages and innumerable closets. Provisions, armories, living quarters. Freight elevators for all kinds of guns and cannons. The supermutant has entrenched himself in some kind of a command center and is busy preparing for the defense of his realm. He must have been warned by somebody.'

'By whom?'

'Perhaps Seiko can tell us. He's listening to their conversations but I have no contact with him.'

Rhodan deliberated for a few seconds. 'Fine, Sengu. Keep up your observations. Try to establish communication with the other mutants, especially with Seiko. Let us know when something new happens. We'll attack in exactly 30 minutes. Keep in the background and intervene only after the main danger is over. Is that clear?'

'Perfectly, sir.'

Rhodan pulled himself up to his full height. 'I'll direct the attack from the auxiliary vessel *Good Hope V*.'

Bell reacted in astonishment. 'From the Guppy?' he wondered. 'And what am I supposed to do with the *Stardust*?'

'Watch out that nothing goes wrong, my friend,' Rhodan comforted him. 'You keep off to the side and make sure that this scoundrel doesn't get away from us. Don't forget he has still at least two destroyers that can travel at the speed of light. He stole three from us; one was destroyed. One is propably located on Mars. That leaves one. And this is the one you have to watch out for.'

'Me too?' chirped Pucky. He didn't look too pleased.

'You too!' Rhodan reassured the little fellow. Then he turned to Bell and patted him on the shoulder. 'I'm glad that we didn't bring our Arkonide friends along for this action. Thora and Khrest are not in favor of war-like activities. They regard them as barbarian manifestation of violence.'

'They aren't too far off, I'd say,'

Rhodan smiled wryly, 'No argument from me, Reg, but can you suggest an alternate solution in this case?'

Bell did not reply; there was none to make. The two men, accompanied by Pucky their trusty follower, returned to the command center. Here Bell took over the command of the *Stardust* while Rhodan hurried to the antigravelevators that would take him to the hangars where he would take care of getting the *Good Hope V* ready for action.

Five minutes later the spacesphere with a diameter of 180 feet left the gigantic *Stardust* and quickly descended into the Earth's atmosphere. The nine destroyers followed in military formation.

The assault on the headquarters of the supermutant was about to begin.

4 FLIGHT OF THE MUTANT MASTER

Hardly had Monterny's direction-finders registered the arrival of the spacesphere and set off the alarm than Rhodan completed his landing manuevers. Only at the very last moment did he brake the scorching descent. The *Good Hope V* was still vibrating on her telescoped supports, hardly 600 feet away from the low flat farm building, when the mutant master opened fire on them.

Out of more than 20 gun barrels roared the flames, over several yards in length, hurling deadly explosive projectiles with terrific impact. The projectiles flew in a straight line toward the *Good Hope V* and detonated on the protective screen which had meanwhile been erected obtaining its energy from the inexhaustible Arkonide reactors. It was a pyrotechnical display never before witnessed by any person living in this quiet landscape in the rocky mountains. Untouched, unscathed by this horrific onslaught stood the spacesphere behind its energy field. It waited.

The automatically controlled defense installations of the mutant master shot off over 500 missiles before the electronic brain realized how useless this procedure actually was. The type of bombardment changed. The mechanical conveyor exchanged the explosive heads of the projectiles. The electronic brain had decided to use atomic weapons.

Rhodan had counted on that. He knew that the protective screen could handle this load by neutralizing it. But the deployment of atomic weapons was an indication that the supermutant had no other means at his disposal now. This was the beginning of the end.

Rhodan waited three to four minutes until a short fire interval occurred. In the meantime he had sufficient opportunity to ascertain the position of the cannons. Their barrels protruded from the bare rock and could in no time disappear beneath the ground where they would be unassailable. If he wished to put these guns out of action he had to act fast.

The fighter robots were ready to be used in battle. The soldiers of the New Power, superbly trained for defensive actions, were feverishly waiting in the large freight lock of the *Good Hope V*. The rest of the mutant corps were impatiently hoping for the go-signal. They alone had some inkling that the final battle could be fought exclusively on a mental level.

Mutants versus mutants!

All the spaceship's available disintegrator cannons were pointed at their targets, ready and waiting. In the instant that Rhodan would cause the energy field to collapse they would discharge their ruinous flood of all-vaporizing rays and annihilate the target. Each crystalline structure would cease to exist.

Rhodan had waited for the short fire-pause. This was one of the shortcomings of a mechanically guided installation, that the various artillery pieces could not be dealt with individually. When they all were silent or had to be exchanged, not a single one was ready to shoot.

The protective energy screen of the *Good Hope V* collapsed.

The same second eight or nine hardly discernible ray-beams shot out of the concave mantle and found their goal. Soil and rocks changed within the fraction of a second into a boiling, vaporizing mass in which the steel cannons were floating about and melting away like so many pats of butter in a frying pan.

Now the ray-beams swung round and aimed at their next objectives. Before the electronic brain of the mutant master's defense installations managed to register the disaster, all the cannons except for two had been disabled. And both these cannons sank through the softened ground into the subterranean shafts. This merely saved them from instantaneous destruction. The energy fingers emerging from the mighty rayguns of the *Good Hope V* melted the exits of the shafts at ground level, forming a glass-like, extremely hard glaze which sealed the pit-mouths absolutely airtight. This eliminated all artillery pieces that the supermutant could have deployed against Rhodan and his men.

And this is what they had been waiting for.

The alarm signal was resounding in shrill tones throughout the ship. Hatches opened. Out of one, a wide ramp descended at a slant toward the ground. Seconds later, twenty Arkonide fighter robots were advancing steadily toward the farm house, nestled among towering trees. The house contained the entrance to the super-mutant's underground fortress. Their left arms were held at an angle. They had no left hands. In their place was a conicalshaped opening which tapered off at the end.

They were followed by the soldiers, armed with handy pulse-ray guns and automatic weapons. Gas grenades were dangling from their belts.

Rhodan had remained in the command center and watched on an observation screen the various phases of the attack. For the time being he didn't dare deploy his mutants; they formed, so to speak, his reserves.

The picture screens had been coordinated in such a fashion that Rhodan was sitting in a glass house. Nothing could be missed by him this way. And thus he was the first to recognize the mutant master's counter measures,

72

which soon became generally noticeable to a disastrous extent.

*   *   *

Clifford Monterny was staring in a blind rage at the controls of his automatically guided cannons. The electronic brain no longer reacted. The needles on the dials pointed to Zero. All his artillery pieces had been canceled out.

But if Rhodan were to believe that he had won the battle, he was sadly mistaken.

Although Clifford Monterny had counted on instantly finishing off any attacker with the concentrated fire of his 20 heavy guns, he had nevertheless calculated the eventuality that he might fail in it. This is where his small but slavishly devoted mutant army came in.

His hands turned a dial on the intercom set. A screen lit up and the head of a Caucasian became visible.

'Roster Deegan,' said the supermutant, 'summon all the other mutants for immediate action. Especially the telekinecists. Rhodan is attacking us with his robots. Under no circumstances must they reach the house. Come here to the command center and direct from here our counterattack.'

Two minutes later Monterny's Telekins entered the fray.

*   *   *

The robots were marching straight ahead, followed by the soldiers.

They had covered about half the distance that had separated them from the house initially. There were another hundred yards till they would reach the farm house, across dried out meadows with occasional groups of trees. Over to one side was a heap of neatly stacked

73

wood logs. The landscape looked peaceful now; there was nothing out of the usual to be seen.

But impressions can be very deceiving.

Rhodan was sitting in the command center of the *Good Hope V*, manning the controls and waiting for further developments. Granted, the defense weapons of the enemy had been silenced, but Monterny had not yet been defeated. A man who has set out to conquer and rule the world does not give up after the first try. He has many aces up his sleeve.

Rhodan wondered what his next maneuver might bring.

The front row of the advancing fighter robots suddenly stopped in their tracks as if they had run into some solid obstacle, an invisible wall. One of the machine men began to stagger, lost his balance and fell flat on his back. He made no attempt to get up. The others – Rhodan couldn't believe his eyes – were lifted off the ground and rose slowly up in the air, hesitantly, in an irregular fashion. Then they started to twist and twirl around their own axis, finally drifting to one side.

Several of the robots began to shoot wildly in all directions. The recoil from their pulse-ray guns pushed them in the opposite direction. They were turning rapidly like pinwheels, sending forth deadly fingers of energy, and drifted back to the ground where a part of their number was rendered harmless by the soldiers.

The second row of robots became the victim of a more skilfully executed assault. Monterny's mutants learned fast. The five robots, marvels of electronics, were hurled through the air by some uncanny force, then slammed violently against the quickly activated protective screen surrounding the *Good Hope V*. Their limp figures crashed to the ground where they remained motionless. Their sensitive inner workings couldn't stand up to such

74

ruthless treatment and tremendous stresses.

But even before the third row of the robots could be incapacitated, something took place which Rhodan had halfway expected.

The soldiers of his little army suddenly began to behave very strangely. Some of the men sat down on the grass, put their dangerous weapons carelessly on the ground next to them and started to unpack their K-rations. Apparently they planned to have a picnic before continuing their mission!

Telekineticist and hypnos, thought Rhodan in mild desperation. Anyhow, Monterny's mutants displayed a certain sense of humor, otherwise they would have ordered these soldiers to kill each other off.

Rhodan prepared instantly for a counter-blow. Its success would depend on whether the supermutant himself had carried out this action or his mutants had. According to Rhodan's experiences to this moment, Monterny was the only living mutant who could repel the effects of the psychobeavers.

Now John Marshall the telepath gave a signal to Tatjana. The young Russian girl, filled with zeal to make up for her previous mistakes, jumped out of the hatch of the *Good Hope V* and ran down the slanting ramp as fast as her legs would carry her. She carried a silver rod in her hand, which she pointed in a direction that clearly indicated how familiar she must be with the underground headquarters of Monterny. She held the rod at a wide angle, pointing at a spot left and front of the house.

Rhodan watched Tatjana on the picture screen. He enlarged the image and could almost read her thoughts from the expression on her face. But John Marshall was able to directly enter her mind and learn from the source what mental commands she was issuing.

Her endeavors were crowned by success in barely one minute. It was amazing to witness what was taking place.

The robots who were still floating in the air lost their invisible support and fell to the ground. Most got quickly back on their feet again. As if nothing had happened, they continued advancing on the house, firing steadily out of their left weapon-arms and shortly reducing the building to a smouldering rubble heap.

The feasting soldiers abruptly stopped their little snack, stared dumbfounded for the fraction of a second at their opened tin cans, dropped everything, seized their weapons and ran after the marching robots.

Tatjana stooped for a moment, the while making sure that Monterny's mutants could no longer exert any influence on their attackers. She realized, however, that the most difficult and dangerous task was still ahead of her. Of course, she didn't know all the details of the mutant master's headquarters, and she had no idea how many people were housed here underground in the passages and chambers hewn from the rock, but she guessed that Monterny would have ready a few more tricks for an unpleasant welcome for his attackers.

She had to find a way of persuading one of the mutants to open the second access route to the underground fortress. She was sure she would be able to manage that with the help of the psychray.

Robots and soldiers came to a halt in front of the smoking ruins of the farmhouse. There was nothing for them to do here. Supposing the entrance to the subterranean labyrinth had been inside the destroyed farmhouse, it was unusable. Nobody could now enter or exit.

Tatjana loosened slightly the screening block around her brain to permit her to absorb the thoughts of other people. She concentrated on the familiar thought pattern of the supermutant and tried to establish communication with him. At the same time she kept her psychobeam pointing constantly in the direction of Monterny's command center; she was ready at any moment to close the block screen once more around her brain.

And then Monterny's voice, weakened to some extent by the residual protective barrier around her brain, was suddenly inside her head. 'Tatjana, you've disobeyed my orders and betrayed our good cause. You've joined the camp of the most despicable enemy of all mankind and ...'

'Enough!' Tatjana concentrated and flung back a denial. She felt fortified by the knowledge that John Marshall could 'hear' her and would transmit the entire conversation directly to Perry Rhodan. 'All you say and all your work consists of empty phrases which serve to hide your true motive: violence. I've seen through you, Clifford Monterny. You have abused my idealism.'

'You fool!' countered the supermutant without attempting to influence Tatjana with his hypnotic suggestions. He knew better: she was impervious to his powers. 'You haven't a chance of overcoming my mutants.'

'Rhodan's weapons are superior, Monterny. His mutants are far more capable than yours and he also has more of them. Give up!'

A wave of soundless, derisive laughter raced through Tatjana's and Marshall's brains.

'Give up?' mocked the supermutant. 'When I give up, the whole world will perish along with me. If Rhodan is to rule over the Earth, then it will be a world without human beings.'

'Thanks,' Tatjana thought calmly. 'You have just spoken your own death warrant. Just try and give a command to your mutants now. We'll see who is the stronger – you or us.'

'Hold on,' begged the mutant master maliciously. 'It's to your advantage to wait. Perhaps you'll succeed in influencing my mutants. But your psychray has no power over me. Nobody can prevent me from issuing a command to my agents the whole world over who have been waiting to carry out their well-planned actions.'

'Possibly,' countered Tatjana. 'But it won't do you much good to issue these commands; you won't be able to establish contact any longer with your agents. They've already been arrested and rendered harmless by the Security Services of the New Power. Don't forget that Rhodan, too, controls a most powerful mutant corps.'

Monterny's thought-curse was more execrable than any spoken words. He betrayed his impotence. And it also told Rhodan that his opponent's strength had been broken. If only they would succeed now in penetrating the underground fortress –

Tatjana didn't waste any time. Her probing thoughts sought and found those of Roster Deegan. Assisted by the psychobeamer she gave him the urgent order: 'Roster, open the emergency exit!'

*   *   *

Monterny could feel that Tatjana was now turning away from him to take up connection with his telekineticist. He guessed what she wanted from him and decided to use this opportunity to put to a test who really was the stronger of the two.

Being a telepath he understood the command she gave Roster. But since he was not only a telepath but a hypno he simply issued a countercommand.

Undecided, Roster stopped in mid-motion: slowly he resumed his seat. The supermutant was stronger than the psychray! Monterny felt triumphant – till abruptly Roster rose again from his chair. Slowly he walked to the door and out into the corridor.

For a moment Monterny stared after him, perplexed, then he cursed and applied his hypnotic power once more and with greater effort. But he noticed at once that his efforts were met by an intensive resistance which he couldn't overcome. He didn't know that meanwhile André Noir, Rhodan's hypno, had combined his forces with Tatjana's. Supported by Tatjana's psychobeamer he, André Noir, was superior to the supermutant.

The fact that he had suffered a defeat had a crushing effect on Clifford Monterny. His technical failure to win the battle against his arch enemy Rhodan didn't especially affect his pride but he simply refused to believe that he should have lost out to him too in a mental contest.

He could have killed Roster but he refrained from doing so for this would have merely resulted in an undesirable reaction of the other mutants who might become critical in view of his current situation. He knew he could keep them in check if they confronted him alone but if they were mentally strengthened by Rhodan's mutants their two forces combined would easily outclass him.

Escape? Flee?

Monterny's lips narrowed to a pencil-thin line. Of course he had already considered such a possibility and had omitted nothing in this respect. His third destroyer was waiting for him in his underground hangar, ready for any eventualities. This ship, barely 90 feet long, could be operated only by himself. Supplies of all kinds were stored aboard. It was well-armed. He could reach the speed of light with this craft. And on the planet Mars waited his last and most horrifying mutant to be used by his master for any action he would deem necessary – however monstrous it might be.

Why then should he wait till he would be up against

the wall without any hope of extricating himself from this situation?

Clifford Monterny made a renewed attempt to regain his influence over Roster Deegan but he soon had to realize that his efforts were in vain. Still he kept persevering. He was determined to give Rhodan as hard a time as possible.

While Roster was opening the emergency exit of the underground fortress and while Tatjana's attention was concentrated on this new task, the supermutant suggested post-hypnotic commands to his mutants and blocked off their brains with psycho-barriers. He knew only too well that it would only be a question of time till these blocks also would collapse again. But this step would insure a longer headstart for him and he desperately needed additional time.

But now he was no longer delaying what had to be done.

He cordoned off his thoughts against the outside world and made sure that even no telepath could be on his trail. Although this caused him at the same time to be completely cut off mentally from his men, it didn't matter to him any longer. He was no longer interested in what would happen in his lost realm. He was now looking ahead; he had a more important task to pursue.

He hurriedly left the command center and ran along the main corridor. From behind he could hear shouts and the sound of shooting reverberating in the many underground passages; somebody was yelling sharp commands. This noise was interspersed with the rhythmical marching steps of the Arkonide fighter robots. Rhodan's forces had successfully invaded the mutant master's domain.

Clifford Monterny clenched his fists in desperate rage, uttered wild curses and hurried on. He turned into one of the many side corridors and increased his speed. If only he had thought earlier to arrange for some underground transportation system! But who'd have considered such a possibility that a seemingly unassailable hiding place would fall at the enemy's first assault? Monterny had to swallow a bitter pill and admit that he had underestimated Rhodan as an opponent.

The corridor seemed to stretch ahead endlessly. It was dimly lit by small lamps in the ceiling that occurred at regular intervals. There were dozens of similar passages and Rhodan's men would need a long time to discover this particular one.

A bend in the corridor. Then another turn. Then the path continued straight ahead.

The supermutant had been clever enough to build his underground hangar sufficiently far from his command center. In case the center would be destroyed during some enemy action, the hangar itself would remain undamaged. Besides, nobody would suspect that Monterny's own emergency exit would be located almost a mile and a half from the main entrance.

The noise coming from behind had died down completely. Monterny slowed down. Heavy beads of perspiration were glistening on his bald head. His puffy features, which had been contorted with hatred and exhaustion, relaxed. The harassed look in his eyes gave way to a familiar expression of icy-cold arrogance. Nevertheless, Monterny was glad that no one could see him now. He, the great mysterious unknown person, who was so far superior to all other mortals, was running for his life, seeking escape in flight!

The corridor ended before a smooth wall.

With trembling fingers Monterny felt along the wall until he found the slight bulge he had been looking for. He greatly pressed down on it; the wall slid up and admitted him to the hangar. The wall closed again behind him.

He was now in a moderate-sized hall, which resembled a shaft. The walls consisted of roughly hewn rocks; ledges and other promontories had been cursorily smoothed over. The rocky ceiling was nearly 300 feet above the floor.

In the middle of this gigantic shaft, resting on its telescope supports, was one of the three destroyers that had been stolen from Perry Rhodan's fleet.

Clifford Monterny breathed a sigh of relief. Not even Rhodan himself could now foil his escape. If right after the takeoff he would accelerate to top speed, nobody would be able to catch up with him.

For a fleeting moment he thought of the abducted scientists who now would be found and released by Perry Rhodan. Monterny felt no regrets for he had made all their specialized knowledge his own; he no longer needed them. They had taught him how to pilot perfectly this stolen spaceship.

In a few strides he reached the telescoped supports and activated the control button of the entrance hatch. Immediately the hatch slid open, many feet above his head, and a ladder emerged and descended toward the floor of the hangar. While this was going on, he ran quickly back to the rock wall, pushed another button hidden in a little depression. Expectantly, Monterny gazed up to the ceiling of the shaft.

The massive rock wall, high above began to move sideways, opening the escape route. Bright daylight filtered down into the hangar.

Clifford Monterny didn't waste any precious seconds. He raced over to the descended ladder and climbed up the rungs. In a few seconds he had disappeared inside the destroyer. The hatch closed with a dull thud.

Long seconds passed. They grew to minutes.

From inside the ship's engine compartment came the roar of the power units and transformers revving up. Highly densified streams of particles were shooting through two-feet thick field conduits, were further compressed in the engines, were accelerated and finally left the glimmering field jets in the ship's rear in the form of fast-as-light, ultra-bright pulse-beams.

The rocky floor underneath the destroyer began to boil while the telescope supports were drawn up. The ship shot upwards.

The energy beams spread in all directions under tremendous pressure, hit the walls of the hangar and melted the solid rock walls. The secret entrance door, leading from the underground labyrinth of corridors into the hangar, was destroyed.

It was obvious : the mutant master had intended to use this escape route only once.

With unbelievable acceleration, the ship shot vertically up and, like a gigantic missile, passed through the 300-foot-long barrel, soon to disappear in the blue depths of the waiting sky.

5 'NO ESCAPE'

Rhodan left the *Good Hope V* – also known as K–5 – the same instant Roster Deegan emerged through the opened emergency exit at the surface. Roster was walking toward Tatjana with a blank stare in his eyes. The young Russian girl approached him and gently tried to restore Deegan's own will, giving it back to him bit by bit.

The mutant corps relieved the robots and the soldiers and were in charge of security. The esper John Marshall stayed near Rhodan and informed him: 'Tatjana reports that there are 10 other mutants besides Deegan in the fortress. A post-hypnotic command forces them to obey the orders of the mutant master. They'll have to be liberated individually from Monterny's influence.'

'How about Monterny's prisoners? What has Tatjana been able to find out about them?'

'No definite news but she believes they're somewhere inside the fortress.'

'Very well, then,' said Rhodan, 'the battle of the mutants can begin! I'll personally take care of Monterny.'

He seized his psychobeamer and advanced toward Tatjana and Deegan, who opposed each other, locked in a silent battle of wills. They were standing near the entrance to the underground fortress. Steps led down into the labyrinth.

'I'll come with you,' Marshall said. He had kept close to Rhodan. 'Also Sengu, Anne Sloane and Betty Toufry. Sengu can warn us of any impending danger while the two telekins can immobilize any attackers until we can break their hypnoblock.'

At this moment the hypnoblock was breaking inside Roster Deegan. The American shook his head as if he had just surfaced from deep water and was suddenly feeling free from the pressure of the deeps. He took Tatjana's hand. 'I still don't quite understand everything but I'm beginning to get some idea of what has happened. Count on me. Set the others free as well, please!'

Rhodan joined their little group. 'Come along, Tatjana. We mustn't waste any time. Nobody knows what devilish tricks the mutant master still has up his sleeve.'

Roster regarded Rhodan quizzically; their eyes met and then he held out his hand. 'You must be Rhodan. I recognize you from pictures. I presume you'll be interested in increasing the numbers of your mutants. In that case there are 10 more mutants waiting down there in the fortress who would be proud to join your forces. But — they aren't free yet.

Tatjana pointed to both Rhodan's psychobeamer and her own. 'It won't be long now,' she promised.

In one of the corridors, on their way to the command center, they encountered the first telekineticist.

Rhodan suddenly was flung to one side. If he hadn't reacted instantly by a reflex and stretched out both hands he would have crashed into the wall head first. He slipped to the ground, trying to make himself as inconspicuous as possible and thus escape the direct line of vision of the fortress' defender. Then calmly he pointed his hypno-rod toward the shadowy figure, which stood out very indistinctly against the poorly lit background.

He directed a powerful barrage of urgent commands at the man's hypnoblock with very little success. Not until André Noir joined forces with him and broke through the existing barrier by exerting tremendous hypnotic pressure, then implanted his counter orders in the mutant's brain, did the mutant master's power over this man give way.

Rhodan, prudently, then gave the man a post-hypnotic command with the help of the psychobeamer. Now was not the time for long explanations.

Step by step they penetrated farther into the super-mutant's realm, now deserted by him. They encountered bitter resistance from the mutants who were still under Monterny's spell. But little by little, Rhodan's and Noir's combined efforts removed this obstacle.

Including Roster, they found 10 mutants altogether who were soon willing to switch allegiance from the tyrannical mutant master and join Rhodan's mutant corps. However their number should have been 11.

Where was the eleventh mutant?

And where was the supermutant himself?

Rhodan looked around. 'Ras Tschubai?' he inquired.

The powerfully built figure of the giant African drew near. 'Yes, sir?'

'Have you searched all the rooms?'

The teleporter raised his hand in an uncertain gesture. 'I couldn't tell for sure. This warren has so many corridors, passages and rooms that it's impossible for me to say whether I have been in every one of them or not. I have definitely located the command center; it was empty. Not a trace of that bald-headed fellow.'

'And how about the scientists?'

Before Ras could answer, Sengu the seer interjected. 'They are imprisoned in a dungeon – an entire complex with regular cells. There's an elevator leading down there.' The Japanese fixed his eyes on a spot on the floor to indicate the direction. Trying to imagine that he could clearly see through solid rock, one couldn't help but shudder in awe. 'Somebody seems to have located them – I can see a figure that's trying to force open the entrance door leading into the prison complex. I can't quite make out who it could be.'

Betty Toufry, both telepath and telekin, joined the little group around Rhodan. 'I'm receiving the thoughts of a man,' she whispered and glanced uncertainly in the same direction as Sengu. 'His thoughts are rather weak and confused. He wants to kill.'

Ras Tschubia turned to Sengu. 'Describe the location of the dungeon, I want to catch that man before he causes a disaster. Hurry, please!'

There was nothing much Rhodan could do here. He just watched passively and gave free rein to his own mutants. He couldn't see, hear or feel anything. Rhodan was not a mutant but a very normal human being – quite apart from certain characteristics which however had nothing to do with structural changes in the brain.

Ras Tschubai listened as Sengu specified the exact location. Then the African teleporter nodded briefly – and vanished.

Those that remained behind felt the slight breeze caused by the air rushing into the vacuum created by the teleporter during and after his rematerialization. At this very same instant, Ras Tschubai materialized again in his own body, exactly at the desired spot he had concentrated on.

Rhodan wanted to make use of this time during Ras' absence. 'Tatjana and Marshall, accompany me. We must find out where Monterny is now. I can't imagine he'd crawl into a corner and wait till we find him. He's not the passive type.

'This fortress has dozens of passages. None of us has seen all of them,' observed Tatjana. 'But I do know, one of these corridors leads to a hangar hewn out of the solid rock. And in this hangar is hidden one of your stolen destroyers. Perhaps Monterny has meanwhile . . .'

'No doubt,' Rhodan said sharply. It was one of the

rare occasions when he briefly lost his temper. 'You should have told me that sooner. I'm convinced the super-mutant is smart enough to realize immediately when he is defeated. But ... say that again! There's a hangar in the underground rock walls?'

'Yes.'

'That means it's to the west. It shouldn't be too difficult to discover the right corridor leading to that hangar. Come along!'

Rhodan hurried ahead through the empty passages, followed immediately behind by Tatjana and Marshall. The sound of their steps was echoed back from the solid walls with a hollow thud.

They arrived at a fork in the road. Rhodan quickly checked his watch compass and chose the outer branch to the left. 'This path runs due west – it could be the right one.'

He didn't wait for a reply but ran on.

From farther ahead suddenly came a dull vibration in the rocks. The floor was shaking under their feet, reminding them of the temblor of a mild earthquake.

Rhodan stopped in his tracks. Marshall grew pale. Tatjana lowered her hand with the hypno-rod in it. 'What was that?' she whispered barely audibly. Rhodan clenched his fist. 'Our destroyer – at least we know now that we chose the right way. 'We've come too late. Maybe our men above-ground are more watchful. Let's have a look at least at that mess!'

Thirty feet before the spot where the corridor formerly ended abruptly in a blank wall, they encountered a dry heat-wave which prevented them from going on. In the dim light coming from the poor lamps in the ceiling Rhodan saw on the ground and on the ceiling stalactites and stalagmites consisting of first molten and then congealed rock. A sudden insight flashed in his brain: of course, the hangar was behind that blind wall in the rocks!

'The heat generated as the destroyer was taking off couldn't dissipate into the atmosphere as is usually the case during blastoffs. It melted the walls instead. I hardly believe we can get through from here into the hangar.' He reflected for a few seconds then added with resignation in his voice: 'It wouldn't do us any good anyhow. Monterny is already racing through space. We can only hope somebody up there noticed his escape.'

'Shouldn't we inform the *Stardust* of his flight?' suggested Marshall.

'Even that would be too late,' said Rhodan with a bitter smile, 'but don't worry, Marshall. In the long run Monterny can't get away from us. We have some idea where he might try to escape to.'

And before Rhodan's inner eye came the vision of the desolate loneliness of a reddish desert, crossed by broad strips of green vegetation. A lonely world only sparsely heated by a far distant sun.

6 PUCKY DARES THE IMPOSSIBLE

Pete Maros was a Mexican but he had very little in common with his original ancestors.

One trait, however, he had definitely inherited from his forefathers, was his volatile temper, which was in sharp contrast with the cool disposition of the Englishman Ray Gall. Ray was the radio man of the destroyer Z-82 which had been taken over by Rhodan after its repair.

Commander of the ship was Julian Tifflor, for the time being still cadet of the Space Academy.

The group of the new destroyers had fanned out and stood not quite 20 miles above the State of Utah. Another 30 miles higher up Reginald Bell comforted himself with the thought that in certain sense he now represented Perry Rhodan's headquarters and had to watch out for the safety of the *Stardust*. Under no circumstances would he risk endangering the giant spacesphere.

Both Tiff and Bell were preoccupied by the same thoughts. 'Here we are dangling high up in the sky and can't even watch what's going on down there below the clouds. Even radio contact has been interrupted – or have you been able to hear anything, Pete?'

The mechanic pointed to the door of the radio cabin. 'Ray hasn't budged from the spot. Let me check.'

The Englishman sat without moving in front of his silent receiving set, dozing. The picture screen which could establish direct communication with the *Stardust* was dark.

'I'd let you know the moment something happens,' grunted Ray. 'That set has been deader than a doornail.'

Ray shut his eyes again.

Pete noted with relief that at least his ears seemed to be wide open. He left the radio cabin and returned to the command center.

Meanwhile Tiff had switched over to magnification of the scanning tele-camera and pointed the lens straight toward the surface of the Earth. There were no clouds to obscure his view. Within a few seconds Tiff could see the entire state of Utah like a map on his observation screen. The magnification increased automatically. The map grew hazy and as soon as it showed up again with sharp outlines it had shrunk to a smaller section but still in the same dimensions. This process repeated itself several times until finally Tiff could clearly recognize the round spot marking the destroyer K-5, landed next to the destroyed farm house.

Tiff remembered Rhodan's instructions: don't bother watching what happens around the K-5, concentrate on the area surrounding the farmhouse and the airspace above Utah.

Tiff sighed. Well, so what else would he do now, even if nobody actually could check up on what he was doing? But anyhow ...

Slowly he moved the objective of the camera toward the west where the high mountains were. Not a very pleasant landscape, he thought. What kind of person would ever have the desire to settle there. Jagged rocks and sharp rocky ridges jutted out from the dense bush. In between were the steep and deep clefts of the canyons cutting through the wildly romantic and irregular terrain.

He was struck at once by the regular outlines of a mountain. It didn't fit into this landscape.

On a relatively flat plateau, covered by a growth of low bushes which was surrounded by steep rocks, he noticed a small, lone mountain. Here by accident? Although it

91

consisted mainly of boulders and rubble, it showed plentiful traces of fertile soil. Still, there was not a single tree growing there. Only sparse tufts of grass revealed that plant life could exist on this mountain.

The foot of the mountain was bulging out in the shape of a crescent while the opposite side seemed to cave in to the interior.

The mountain looked like a man-made structure; reminded Tiff of a slag heap.

Tiff had come fully alive by now. He had forgotten the meaning of boredom and disappointment. During the briefing session that preceeded the attack, Rhodan had asserted that the area around the mutant master's farmhouse was totally uninhabited. And now Tiff discovered a good mile away from the destroyed ranch a newly raised waste dump.

Pete had stepped over to Tiff and peered over his shoulder. 'Looks like someone was digging for ore there,' he stated.

'And brought all the dirt up to the surface?' asked Tiff.

'Sure. I suppose it's a side shaft of the old mine that used to be somewhere around here.'

'When was that?'

'Last time they were working this mine was some 20 years ago.' Pete recalled what he had been told during their briefing course in Terrania before they left for this mission. 'But they gave it up, it didn't yield enough.'

'That's most interesting,' exclaimed Tiff with a note of triumph in his voice. This seemed to further confirm his suspicions. 'And how can you explain that nothing but a bit of grass, no other vegetation like bushes or shrub has grown on this hill?'

Pete was dumbfounded; he didn't say a thing. He examined the observation screen closer, then remarked: 'You're right, it's real peculiar, Tiff!'

'I'm glad you agree that there's something fishy going on down there. I'd bet that only recently a new ...'

He stopped abruptly in mid-sentence. While talking with Pete, he had not taken his eyes off the strange slag heap. Quite by accident his glance had wandered over to the adjoining plateau and he became aware of a sudden change.

'Look! Over there! At the inner side of the mountain!'

Right next to the suspicious-looking slag heap they saw the rocky ground start to move. A round disk of 90 feet diameter began to shift to one side. Below they could make out a dark opening which was weakly illuminated by a light coming from down below.

A spaceship! A destroyer of the same type as their own – identical to the one that had attacked him near the planet Mars while he was on a training mission.

The spaceship below took off with such tremendous speed that it reached the same altitude as Tiff's and Pete's ship within a few seconds. And in no time it had disappeared in the dark-violet sky.

Something seemed to snap in Tiff; his doubts and hesitant attitude gave way to instant action now. 'Ray, contact the *Stardust* and inform Reginald Bell. We're pursuing the unknown ship.' He swung the drive stick all the way forward for utmost acceleration. The gravity fields were automatically switched on in order to neutralize the sudden jump in G's. 'Pete, man the neutron cannon. Ray is to take up position at the rear guns as soon as he's sent his bulletin to Bell.'

The fugitive ship was lost among the stars and Tiff had to search for minutes before he could locate it again. But since it was the same type of spaceship as his own, he could hardly make up for wasted time and hope to overtake it. Its headstart was too great. All he could hope to do now was to follow on its trail, to keep the same distance at least as soon as both ships would reach maximum speed.

Rapidly the Earth sank away below them, shrinking to the size of a blue globe. Ray emerged from the radio cabin and came to the command center. He sat next to Tiff in the second pilot's seat. 'That was quite some surprise,' he said quickly. 'You should have heard Reginald Bell! He ordered us to find out the eventual destination of the unidentified ship. Could be the destroyer stolen by the supermutant with him in it, trying to escape. As soon as Bell gets a confirmation from Rhodan whether his assumptions are justified, he'll follow behind us. He'll get in touch with us, he promised, 'in order to let us know.'

Tiff kept his eyes glued to his radar screen. The blip didn't change size now. He read the range indicator which showed that the fugitive was about 1200 miles ahead of Tiff's craft, his ship constantly accelerating and would soon reach one-fourth the speed of light.

Tiff looked out of the tiny window. Before him stretched the infinity of the universe with all its marvels and dangers. And up ahead, hidden among the myriads of stars, a pinpoint of light was speeding toward its unknown distant destination.

It hit him like a ton of hot bricks when he once again looked at his observation screen.

The spot had grown in size.

The other ship was now only 300 miles away.

It had reduced its speed.

*   *   *

Ras Tschubai materialized less than three feet away from the mutant stranger, who whirled around in fright and stared at the sudden apparition as if it were a ghost.

He was a Japanese, a stocky, rather young man whose right forefinger was crooked around the trigger of an automatic pistol. But he held his weapon pointing to the ground and made no attempt to use it.

Ras suspected that the young Japanese was waiting for new instructions but apparently none were coming. However he was still subjected to a hypnotic spell which robbed him of his individual freedom of movement and decision.

Two yards farther on there was a door, locked by a magnetic mechanism. Behind it, Ras knew, were the living quarters of the imprisoned scientists.

Swiftly he lept over to the Japanese and relieved him of his weapon. His rapid action took the young fellow so completely by surprise that he couldn't offer any resistance.

Ras seized the automatic and shoved it between his belt and uniform. 'Open the door to the quarters of the scientists!' he ordered the Japanese.

At this moment a noise came up from behind. He could hear approaching steps. He turned around and by the light of a dim little ceiling lamp he recognized Rhodan and Tatjana. They obviously must meanwhile have found the elevator and have come down with it.

Ras breathed a sigh of relief. He raised his arm and waved to both Rhodan and Tatjana. At this very instant Monterny's post-hypnotic suggestion grabbed hold again of the young Japanese mutant. Ras saw Rhodan and Tatjana simultaneously raise their psychobeamers and point them in his direction. He received the absolutely nonsensical command not to attack Ras Tschubai – to refrain from attacking himself.

This command was, of course, intended for the Japanese mutant who was just about to hurl himself against the huge African. However, he stopped midway and, totally perplexed, put his hands to his forehead – and then sank like a sack slowly to the ground. The excessive

strain on his tortured brain had rendered him uncon-
scious.

The pressure in Ras Tschubai's head ceased; he turned
around and saw the Japanese lying limp as a rag on the
floor. Rhodan and Tatjana hurried over to him. 'Two
psycho-rayguns at a time is a bit too much for anybody,'
explained Rhodan. 'Maybe if that idea had occurred to
us sooner we might not have lost the Supermutant.
Where are the prisoners?'

Ras motioned toward the heavy iron gate. 'Over there.'

And – then he vanished. It took hardly 10 seconds until
he reappeared. He smiled and seemed a bit confused.
Rhodan scrutinized his face and asked, quite worried by
Tschubai's peculiar expression. 'What's the matter, Ras?
Are the prisoners . . .?'

'They are in there alright,' the African reassured him,
still shaking his head in disbelief. 'But these scientists
are some mighty peculiar creatures. I materialized inside
the lab of one of the physicists. Do you think that fellow
was in the least frightened when I suddenly appeared
there like a ghost from nowhere? Not a bit. He hardly
looked up when I suddenly stood beside him and
watched him as he studied some of his plans. He simply
gestured with his hand as if he wanted to shoo me away
like a bothersome insect and mumbled something like
"Come back again in 10 minutes, will you?" '

Rhodan grinned and turned to Tatjana. 'I bet anything
that was the world-famous professor Glenner; sounds
just like him.' But then Rhodan grew serious again and
said to Ras : 'Open that gate. We can't afford the time to
wait for Glenner to be willing to see us. He can continue
his work in Terrania.'

Ras walked over to the door.

* * *

Destroyer Z-82 closed in on the fleeing spaceship. They were already eight million miles away from Earth and the distance increased steadily. Their speed was constant. A radio message from Bell informed them that the *Stardust* had been ordered to take up pursuit. At least they were supposed to find out where the Supermutant planned to escape to.

Pete's face had a pensive expression. 'If we want to finish off that monster we'll have to be quick about it. Otherwise Bell will beat us to it and grab all the credits too. I know him very well.'

Tiff bestowed a reprimanding glance on the Mexican. 'I'd be ashamed if I were you even to entertain such thoughts. The mutant master is the enemy of the entire world and it doesn't matter a bit who finishes him off – the main thing is he'll be rendered harmless. Ray, try to make radio contact with the ship ahead.'

'You know, there's a direct line to the radio cabin. You can talk to that ship from right where you are this way.'

Tiff made the necessary connections, switched various levers, called the Supermutant in the fleeing ship ahead on the usual telecom wave, then waited at intensive reception. Hardly 10 seconds passed before the face of the world enemy appeared on the glowing picture screen. His bald head was shining like a polished billiard ball. He wore a smug expression. His small eyes, deeply imbedded in cushions of fat, were glowering threateningly. He was obviously highly interested as he studied intensely his pursuers. He took his time, looking them over calmly one after the other as if he planned to engrave their images on his brain forever.

Tiff felt an icy shower running down his spine while he was under the scrutiny of the monster. He was sure his friends must have the same reaction.

'What do you want from me?' asked the Supermutant

with uncanny composure. He didn't give away, not even with the slightest bat of an eyelash, that in reality he felt defeated.

Tiff collected his wits. 'Give up the fight, Monterny,' he said. 'Your fortress in Uath has fallen and your mutants are in the custody of Perry Rhodan. You haven't the ghost of a chance. The battleship of the New Power will arrive here any minute now.'

The icy-cold eyes smiled threateningly. 'You are a fool, young man. Do you really believe I let you approach this close to my ship in order to listen to a lecture from you? Are you seriously considering I would ever dream of surrendering? You underestimate me and my intentions, my friend. Maybe you don't know it yet but I'll let you in on a little secret. I am quite capable – thanks to this television contract – to ascertain your brain-wave pattern. Your name is Julian Tifflor, right? And your two companions are Pete Maros and Ray Gall. I'm sure you already have guessed what's going to happen from now on: You'll do exactly what I order you to do. All I need is a slight headstart. So in the meantime you'll delay Rhodan's battleship a little. That should be enough to find a hiding place for me somewhere in this solar system. But please tell Rhodan for me that I'll return some day. And not alone!'

Tiff's hand shot forward. The videoscreen grew suddenly dark.

Then Tiff stared at the pale faces of his companions.

The same instant a mighty fist seemed to smash out his conscious awareness.

*   *   *

Bell and Major Nyssen, commander of the interceptors stationed aboard the *Stardust*, sat in the command center of the giant spacesphere, watching intently the magnifying frontal observation screen.

'Strange guy, that Tifflor,' remarked Nyssen. 'Why is he slowing down?'

Bell didn't take his eyes off the screen on which truly odd events began to take shape. The spaceship of the fleeing mutant master started to accelerate again and raced out into deep space. Its nose pointed in the direction of the asteroid belt and ignored the planet Mars over to the right.

Destroyer Z-82 on the other hand kept braking its course and swung around in a wide turn to resume its flight exactly in the opposite direction from before. Its nose was pointing now directly at the *Stardust*, which had taken off from Earth in pursuit of the two spaceships.

'Tifflor has given up?' murmured Bell, surprised, and narrowed his eyes. 'That doesn't fit in at all with the picture I have of this promising young cadet. And Monterny can't be behind Tiff's sudden odd behaviour. He knows neither Tiff nor the other two men aboard the Z-82.'

It would have been an easy thing for the *Stardust* to execute a small space jump in order to overtake the fugitive Monterny in his stolen ship but it was not feasible in the case of relatively short stretches to carry out absolutely correctly this jump across the intended distance. And in normal space even the mighty battleship of the Arkonides could not surpass the speed of light. Bell, however, thought he knew where the Supermutant was fleeing to and that reassured him somewhat. His foremost concern was therefore concentrated on the Z-82 and its crew.

The destroyer was rushing at incredible speed straight toward the *Stardust*. When the two spaceships were separated by only 30 miles the Z-82 began to blast away, its pulse-ray cannon aiming at the giant spacesphere. In the meantime Bell had reduced the speed of his ship to facilitate maneuvring the craft. An energy screen had been erected around the *Stardust* to protect it against the oncoming assault.

The pulse-rays of the destroyer hit against this protective screen, gliding off its sides, only later to glance off into space, having totally failed to cause any damage to the *Stardust* as intended.

Shortly before the Z-82 would have reached the spacesphere, the smaller ship pulled steeply upward, then looped the loop and returned to renew its senseless maneuver!

Bell, shaking his head, said to Nyssen: 'We have to put him out of action otherwise he won't give up attacking us. How the Supermutant managed to bring Tiff under his control is an absolute mystery to me. But there's no doubt he somehow got to him. And as long as Tifflor isn't shocked out of his hypnotic spell, he'll represent a constant danger to our safety. He'll fly back to Earth and attack any of our ships. Some might not be forewarned and fall victim to his assault or perhaps destroy him. And that's exactly what Monterny has been counting on. He knows we won't leave Tiff in a lurch – and abandon him to his fate. This will get us off his back for enough time to make good his escape. I only wonder how we can get some sense back into Tifflor?'

'Hypno-rod,' muttered Nyssen. 'You should give it a try.'

'Pretty hopeless, Nyssen. Even if there are no obstacles between the rod and the target, and if you apply it over a very short distance only, it is quite difficult to wrench someone out of a hypnoblock. But in this case the rays would have to pass twice through the heavy walls of the two spaceships and besides they would have to go through two energy fields. No, not a ghost of a chance, believe me.'

100

'What do you think of the idea if we'd shoot his ship's rear section to pieces? As long as he remains inside the command center no harm will come to him. But this way he won't have the energy source to continue his attacks on us.'

'Not a bad idea if everything else fails,' Bell admitted while trying feverishly to come up with a better suggestion. True, the total loss of a destroyer was easier to bear than three people losing their lives. But it would be better if this alternative could be avoided altogether.

Bell scratched his head.

'When will you finally think of asking *me* for help?' came an almost pitiful sounding, squeaky little voice. The mouse-beaver sat on his hind legs, using his broad tail for additional support. The guileless eyes of the little animal displayed such expectancy and willingness to help that Bell would have loved to bend down and pet the little guy. But he controlled his urge.

Instead he put on officious airs and asked, 'What kind of help for instance?'

Pucky shook his little head, regretfully it seemed, and grinned. 'I'd like to play a few games. It's been such a long time, you know.'

Bell knew only too well what Pucky meant by 'playing.' The mouse-beaver was a telekin and whenever he made use of his supranormal abilities he called that 'playing'. In the early days of their acquaintance this had led to many a calamity and one time, Bell recalled now in a flash, even the steering controls of the *Stardust* had fallen victim to Pucky's passion for 'playing', with the unpleasant result that the ship had been hurtled through hyperspace over a distance of many light-years from their intended destination.

'Playing games?' grunted Bell pensively. A vague plan was already taking shape in his brain. 'If you stick absolutely to the rules I might consider it. You know that Rhodan has expressly forbidden you to play without his special authorization ...'

'I know!' Pucky raised his furry little paws with a dramatic gesture. 'But seeing as I'm now the only mutant on board this ship – and both a telekin and a teleporter – that means I'm the only one who can put the destroyer out of action without annihilating it.'

Nyssen intervened. 'Pucky's right, he should put the reactor out of commission.'

'Okay, then,' said Bell. 'Pucky, have major Nyssen explain to you how to disconnect a reactor.'

'It's really quite simple when all is said and done,' the commandant of the interceptor began eagerly. 'You must push the separating isolation wall between the two drive elements. It's possible to do that by remote control from the command center. The process can be guided and regulated as needed. So it won't help us very much to only interrupt the connection between the reactor and the command center. Tifflor is intelligent enough to quickly fix this faulty functioning. But if we induce some change inside the reactor itself which can't be affected by any manipulation from the control room, then Tiff's hands will be tied, he'll be helpless. The destroyer won't receive the necessary energy supply and the ship can no longer be maneuvered.'

'How about the emergency batteries?' inquired Bell.

'They'll just do for the lights throughout the destroyer and running its communication system. There's not much else he can do with them, definitely not as a power supply for the whole craft.'

Pucky waddled over to the little cabin window and peered through it in order to observe the approaching destroyer which was once again shooting off deadly pulse-rays. He shook his dainty head with an almost human gesture. 'I'll need the exact location of the reactor,' he piped.

Nyssen took a piece of paper and made a sketch. It showed the position of the reactor in the last third of the destroyer. On another sheet of paper the major explained the reactor and its construction.

'Look here, Pucky, here's a chamber containing both elements. There's the separating wall. It's held in place by small but very intensive magnetic fields. If your strength is sufficient you can push the wall down between the two elements. All that's needed then would be for you to bend one of the poles or break it off. No force in the universe could lift the dividing barrier up again and restore the reactor to its proper working order.'

Pucky bared his single, big incisor tooth. 'Except for me, of course,' he chirped triumphantly. Then he added, 'don't worry, I'll make it alright. Just give me enough time now to concentrate properly. Maks sure nobody disturbs me.'

Bell swallowed hard. He held back a fittingly sarcastic remark, knowing better than to antagonize the little fellow. He stared in fascination at the picture screen where the Z-82 was visible.

Tiff was about to start another onslaught and came closer with unbelievable acceleration.

*   *   *

A message kept hammering inside Tiff's brain : *this gigantic spacesphere is your enemy. You must attack it over and over again! You must delay in until the mutant master has safely escaped!*

Tiff could think clearly and from time to time he would brood over the puzzling question why suddenly Rhodan should be his enemy and why the Supermutant had become his ally. But he couldn't arrive at an answer – he just kept attacking the *Stardust*.

Like obedient automatons Pete and Ray handled the weapons which belonged to the destroyer's equipment. They hurtled dis-rays and pulse-rays ceaselessly against their target, the huge *Stardust*, hovering motionless in space. The two cadets didn't realize that a single energy thrust from the giant sphere would suffice to shatter their own energy screen and also could easily annihilate them together with their Z-82.

They were setting out on the twentieth attack!

Z-82 had turned around once more and was racing with constant speed toward its target. Upstairs in the tower Pete was pushing the firing buttons of the cannons. Ray was sitting at the rear raygun waiting until the Z-82 would swing around for its return flight.

But this time nothing happened.

Destroyer Z-82 kept on its course going straight toward the *Stardust* without any action from its artillery pieces.

Tiff didn't notice this change at once; he was concentrating too much on advancing toward the spacesphere as close as possible, in order to increase the effectiveness of the death-dealing rays. Not until the very last moment did he let the helm-jets come into play so that Ray would also have a chance to shoot off a thrust of fire at the opponent.

Tiff moved the steering lever to the right but Z-82 remained on the same course.

The slender craft raced straight toward the protective energy screen of the *Stardust*, collided with it at an obtuse angle and was propelled forward with almost no change of direction. The impact imparted a slight spin to the destroyer. Tumbling slowly, the Z-82 was gliding into the space between Mars and Earth. The energy supply was completely cut off. The artificial gravitational fields that were used to neutralize the increase in G's failed completely. Tiff was thrown out of his seat when the ship hit the *Stardust*'s energy field. He sailed clear through the control center till he hit his head against a brace. He was knocked out for a second. Then he realized with amazement that he had become weightless.

Pete and Ray more or less shared his fate. The Mexican was suspended from the ceiling, head downwards, trying all the time in vain to reach the firing button of his cannon in order to continue with the senseless shooting. Ray was not quite as lucky. He toppled over sideways from his chair and hit his head against the controls of his neutron-beamer. He lost consciousness immediately.

Bell observed on his screen how Tiff's ship was drifting off into space. Then he turned to the little mouse-beaver, who had just returned from his mission.

Pucky looked none the worse for the tremendous strain he had just gone through when he teleported himself back and forth between the *Stardust* and the Z-82 and deployed his telekinetic skills.

The mouse-beaver rubbed his little nose with his paw and yawned loudly. Suddenly he gave out a whistling sound, grinned, very pleased with himself, and bared his lonely incisor. 'It was pretty difficult,' he admitted; 'I'd like to know who thought up that barrier installation in that reactor. I could hardly move it.'

'But you made it alright!' Bell was triumphant. He bent down to gently rub his little friend's brown fur. 'Tiff's ship has no energy supply at all. Unless we pick him up and rescue him he'll drift in for a little visit to the planet Pluto.'

Major Nyssen pointed at the observation screen. He seemed quite worried. 'It's high time we get to them.'

'Don't be too alarmed, we'll bring them back to the *Stardust* and anchor their ship outside. Then we'll get those poor devils under Dr. Manoli's care as fast as we

105

can. He'll teach them quickly again who's their friend and master.'

And with stupendous acceleration the giant space-sphere set out on its chase after the helplessly drifting Z-82.

7 ULTIMATUM

Allan D. Mercant left his headquarters rather unwillingly but Rhodan's invitation to come to Terrania had sounded very official and urgent. Mercant was under the impression that he wasn't the only one to be invited there. Later on it turned out that he was correct in this assumption.

Within a few hours the jet carried him to Asia. As he was arriving at the airport of Terrania, climbing on stiff legs out of the cabin and then walking the short stretch to the barrier gate, another machine came in for a landing. Five minutes later he recognized the lone passenger of that machine as the President of the Asiatic Federation. There was no reception committee for either Mercant or the president to welcome them on their arrival. Now the president strode over to Mercant, his face clearly expressing his surprise.

'You –?' the Chinese murmured while his perplexity rose. Then he narrowed his eyes to a slit and stretched out his hand in greeting to the Chief of the Terranian Defense Federation. 'So you received an invitation too.'

'Would I have come here otherwise?' replied Mercant and shook hands with the other man. 'I didn't want to miss the important disclosures Rhodan promised us.'

The President of the AF, a husky, tall Chinese, shook his head. 'They haven't even found it necessary to come and get us from the airport. Or are we supposed to walk on foot from here to Terrania?'

'There are plenty of taxis outside,' Mercant enlightened him, remembering his last visit to the capital city of the New Power. 'Could be that Rhodan wants to avoid any notice of our coming.'

'Then let's go. I hope I've enough change on me to pay for the taxi,' remarked the Chinese.

'They're free of charge here in Terrania,' Mercant reassured him.

The Chinese pressed his narrow diplomat's satchel tightly under his arm and started to move in the direction of the exit.

'I'm quite surprised though,' said Mercant, 'that there isn't as much traffic here at the airport as usual. It looks half asleep. There's hardly anyone around.'

An Arkonide service robot was sitting at the gate and let them pass without checking on them. Mercant presumed that their brain-wave patterns must have been programmed in the automaton's positronic brain. That meant that their arrival and reception had been planned in all details.

But why then no reception committee such as always welcomed VIP's?

Mercant decided to drop the subject. Rhodan did nothing without having a valid reason behind it. There must have been some weighty motivation for his behavior. While they were walking across the wide square toward the waiting cabs, Mercant recalled once more the text of the invitation. It had been quite brief and to the point:

Allan D. Mercant, Chief of the TDF. You are herewith requested to take part in an extraordinary session of the New Power and the rest of the various terrestrial power blocs. This meeting will clear up many vital questions for all concerned parties.

Perry Rhodan
President of the New Power

A taxi driver opened the door for them, waited until they had got into the cab. Then he brought them by the fastest route to the modern metropolis. Mercant's attempt to start a conversation with the driver failed. The man simply would not reply. Besides he acted as if he had no idea that his passengers were quite prominent people.

Mercant soon forgot his problems. Beneath them lay the most modern city in the world with its towering skyscrapers, wide ribbons of roads and the gigantic green recreational spaces. Flying very low the aircab crossed the central square of the city, which was framed on all four sides by the official government buildings of the New Power.

The square wasn't empty today.

To Mercant's utmost astonishment he observed that a regular army had lined up on parade down there. There wasn't too much he could recognize from up above but still he could make out not only soldiers but also heavy artillery pieces. In between were armored tanks with their impenetrable Arkonite hulls.

With very alert eyes the Chinese regarded the military spectacle. He cleared his throat and spoke to Mercant. 'I wonder whether there is any connection between this display and our meeting?'

Mercant shrugged his shoulders. 'I don't know but perhaps Rhodan will be good enough to explain the purpose of this demonstration. But it could also be just a victory parade to honor those men who defeated the Supermutant.'

The corners of the AF president's mouth drooped. 'As far as I can recall, this Supermutant managed to escape. Rhodan conquered merely his hiding place.'

Mercant felt anger rising inside him. 'What do you mean by "merely"? After all, Rhodan was successful in

109

liberating 12 men from the clutches of the so called Supermutant. I'm afraid you don't quite realize in what danger all of us have been. We all owe thanks to Perry Rhodan that he was able to break the mutant master's power.'

'Wasn't the Supermutant Rhodan's enemy and not ours?' suggested the Chinese. Mercant noticed that the taxi was coming in for the landing now. He decided to change the topic. 'Perhaps we'll soon learn more about this affair. Look, we're landing on the Government heliport. That's a sure sign that our pilot here knew all along who his passengers were and where he was supposed to take them. Well, let's let them surprise us.'

They touched down on a circular place covered with white gravel. Here for the first time it became quite obvious that they were being expected. Flanked by two high officers, Reginald Bell advanced in an almost solemn pace, greeted first the President of the AF then – with a glance imploring for understanding – Mercant.

'Gentlemen, you are late. The other guests are already waiting impatiently for you. May I ask you to follow me, please!'

It was actually not a question but a request. Before Mercant could put in a word, Bell turned on his heels and walked ahead of them. The two officers moved to either side of Mercant and the Chinese and led them on, walking behind the Minister of the Security Forces of the New Power.

Mercant used this opportunity to glance swiftly toward the troops which were standing at attention on the central square. One could hardly avoid noticing this powerful display of disciplined might.

With a shock he realized suddenly that the rows upon rows of motionless, quietly waiting soldiers were not genuine soldiers at all. They were glittering robots, each

110

armed with a super heavy hand pulse-raygun. Also the mobile pieces of artillery were manned by robots. There was not a single living soul to be seen on this square.

The uncanny silence and immobility of the unassailable army made such a deep impression on Mercant that he followed after Bell and the President of the AF with an indescribable sense of helplessness. His only hope was that the President of the AF too would sense the implied threat behind this demonstration of the strength of the New Power.

But he quickly revised this view and thought instead: *warning*!

* * *

It was a small and very functional room. One of its walls consisted of an oversized videoscreen which was not on at present. At a semi-circular table sat four men: Mercant and the presidents of the Western and Eastern Blocs and of the Asiatic Federation.

Across from them, and a little higher, were seated five persons. Perry Rhodan in the middle, to his right his representative Colonel Freyt and Bell. To Rhodan's left, the Arkonides Khrest and Thora with impenetrable miens. Thora's reddish eyes rested impassively on the faces of the most powerful men on Earth.

Rhodan's hands were resting on a small box on which 10 red buttons could be seen. Next to each button was a tiny sign with some inscription.

Rhodan lifted his head and contemplated the faces of the four men across the table who looked up to him eagerly and expectantly. There was a fine, hardly observable smile in Rhodan's eyes, mixed with a cold blaze which seemed to contain a warning.

'Gentlemen,' began Perry Rhodan with a friendliness which was in sharp contrast to the atmosphere in the

111

room. 'You've probably been wondering why I invited you to come to this discussion here in Terrania. You are quite justified in doing so. But I won't keep you much longer in suspense. Before I state my demands a few explanations are in order.'

The President of the AF leaned forward. 'Demands?' he said in disbelief and surprise.

Bell grinned sideways at him with a rather friendly smile. Rhodan nodded curtly without moving a muscle in his face. 'Demands – you have heard me correctly, Mr. President. But let this now be your least worry. Right now there are other things of far greater immediate interest to you – and all of you, gentlemen, by the way.'

Rhodan glanced at the little box and pushed a button.

The outsize videoscreen was clearly visible to all; it almost looked like a movie screen. The room was fairly dark so that the three-dimensional color pictures looked lifelike.

The spectators reacted with bewilderment when they recognized what Rhodan planned to show to them. Partially, these events had taken place within their own realms of power and were still quite vivid in their memories.

Strike of the machinists in Detroit, USA.

Revolution in Brazil.

An attempt on the life of the Chief delegate of the Eastern Bloc on the occasion of his visit to London and the resulting diplomatic complications.

Rebellion of the workers in Siberia.

Race riots in the USA.

Rise of the crime rate in Japan.

Famine in China due to the failure of those officials in charge of agriculture and the food industry.

The events were unfolding continuously on the picture screen, without commentary or sound. This heightened the effectiveness of the presentation.

Then the screen darkened again. The four men looked questioningly at Rhodan. Finally the President of the Western Bloc cleared his throat. 'What is all that supposed to mean? We are all familiar with this from our recent news programs and TV reports. I'm sure you haven't had us come all this way here just to show us these news pictures.'

'Quite right!' Rhodan answered and placed his finger on the next button. 'Let's go on.'

What came now were older war pictures from the worldwide conflagrations that had periodically wracked mankind from World War I to the latest atomic conflict which had been nipped in the bud thanks to Rhodan's energetic intervention. These scenes, too, unrolled on the videoscreen without any additional commentary.

Rhodan removed his hand from the little box as soon as the screen grew dark again. He looked straight at the four men. 'You have just witnessed a demonstration of cause and effect. Wars are always caused by some reason or other. If we believe now that we have overcome any future threats of war we are sadly mistaken, as events here have demonstrated so clearly. There are still revolutions, strikes, dissatisfactions and armed conflicts. There is still distrust and suspicion amongst the members of the human race, though we have already crossed the threshold to a new era. You know all this, gentlemen – but you are ignorant of one vital fact: one man alone is responsible for a large part of these causative events. I'm referring to the Supermutant, Clifford Monterny.'

Murmuring and restlessness broke out among the audience which had been so silently attentive all along. Mercant leaned forward and gazed into Rhodan's eyes. There was a deep fold in the middle of his forehead; he opened his mouth as if he wanted to speak but no sound came out.

'The mutant master?' asked an unbelieving president of the Eastern Bloc.

'Yes, he is responsible to a large extent for these catastrophes on Earth. The second guilty party is none other than you, Gentlemen. Yes, you are also to be blamed for all the misery that still rules over mankind. How difficult it is for you to overcome your past; you cannot forget the old ways. However! The mutant master's example has taught us that a divided world may always be at the mercy of an individual if the latter is a positive mutant but endowed with negative character traits. For the time being I have smashed the Supermutant's command center but don't assume that all danger has been removed now. Even if Clifford Monterny should be dead, such a threat will always be hanging over our heads. There will forever arise new supermutants, new slave masters – forever and ever.'

Rhodan pushed once more on another button. The bright videoscreen showed suddenly a true-to-life image of the universe. At first the people viewing the screen could not ascertain which section of the universe this was supposed to represent. But then they recognized a brightly flaring nova.

'That,' said Rhodan with chilling calm, 'used to be a solar system like our own. It too contained only one inhabited planet. Its people were intelligent and vital but also ambitious and narrowminded in a cosmic sense. They constructed the best weapons to fight each other. And then, one day the Topides, a lizard-like intelligent race, found that solar system and attacked and destroyed it. They met with no defense preparations for the native inhabitants had been too busy making each other's lives miserable. Well, they got rid of all worries, their petty squabbles and competitive wars with one fell sweep.'

114

Rhodan pointed at the flaming nova. 'That's all that remained of their sun and the rest of its eleven planets.'

The picture faded away and the screen was dark again.

Breathless silence had fallen over the room.

Rhodan cleared his throat. 'I see you have grasped the meaning of my message. Alright, I'm asking you now: Is that the fate you'd desire for mankind? Do you want our own sun to some day flare up into a nova, ignited by the horrendous powers of an extraterrestrial intelligent race?'

'We are strong enough to ward off any attack,' countered the President of the AF. 'We have weapons . . .'

'True, you have weapons,' Rhodan interrupted sarcastically. He quickly exchanged glances of agreement with Mercant, who was on his side as Rhodan knew. 'But why do you have these weapons? To defend your own Asiatic Federation! Not until you produce arms solely for the defense of all mankind, of all the world, will this make sense. But let's return to the Supermutant for a moment. I've learned from his mutants that he was busy adding fuel to the discord among our nations, was inciting them to riots, caused strikes and headed them towards war. He is a hypno, gentlemen. He took over the will power of influential politicians and used them to his own nefarious ends. He might even have exerted his influence on you. Now that he has fled from our globe, temporarily I assume. I give you this good advice: use this breathing space well. Find new ways to unite the governments of the AF, the Eastern Bloc and the Western Bloc to one single, united force. That is the demand I mentioned earlier! It is not a new request, you must admit. New this time is the limit I am setting for the furfillment of my demand. Unless a World government has become a reality by one year from today, I'll bring about this unification *without* your consent. And I shall use for this purpose all the means I have at my disposal.'

115

Mercant regarded the empty screen. His face was devoid of any expression.

The three presidents had jumped up in unison and stared furiously at Perry Rhodan. When their eyes met his icy cold, determined glance they fell back into their seats. The faces of the two Arkonides showed no emotion whatsoever. Colonel Freyt and Reginald Bell had a hard time suppressing a violent desire to grin.

'We could conduct some preliminary talks,' the President of the Western Bloc moaned painfully. He threw a pleading glance at his two colleagues. 'The organization of a World government ...'

'Is not so difficult,' interrupted Rhodan. 'Just imagine Earth threatened by a gigantic danger. You'd be surprised how fast you'd find a solution then. By the way, I can assure you that this threat is not a figment of my imagination. It is very real, as long as Clifford Monterny is alive and undefeated.'

'We'll think about it,' said the President of the Eastern Bloc.

'Don't think! Act!' Rhodan ordered. 'And this goes for all of you. Get used to the idea it's better to live in harmony some day with all the lizards and spider-like races – or whatever shape the various intelligent life forms in the universe come in. Gentlemen, the final decision of how and under what form the world government will come about rests with you alone. The decision *whether* it will come to pass is mine.' And for the first time Rhodan smiled. 'You may believe me, this decision has already been reached.'

Rhodan motioned to Bell.

The Minister of Security of the New Power rose. 'This concludes our meeting, gentlemen. May I invite you to watch a parade of our troops which has been arranged in your honor. Afterwards, a reception for you has been planned by our diplomatic corps. Later tonight, our jets will return you to your countries. Will you follow me, please!'

Wordlessly the three presidents followed Reginald Bell out of the room. None seemed to notice that Allan D. Mercant remained behind and was led to an adjoining room by Perry Rhodan.

*   *   *

'... which is why its imperative that we don't rest till the mutant master has been rendered harmless or finished off for good, Mercant.' It was Rhodan speaking. 'I myself will stay here on Earth but Reg will resume pursuit of the fugitive. We've already assembled a small fleet for the sole purpose of finding the Supermutant.'

The chief of all the united secret service organizations of the world nodded approvingly but couldn't conceal his skepticism. 'The solar system's immense, Rhodan – how do you propose to find one single individual in it? You've no trail to pursue, no clues – nothing.'

'Ah, but that's not true.' Rhodan smiled and looked at Bell as he entered the room just at this moment. 'We do have a clue. Besides, I'm also counting on the old Axiom that every criminal sooner or later makes a fatal mistake. Clifford Monterny isn't the kind of man to withdraw from the scene as long as he has a trump in his hand.'

'A trump!' Mercant raised his head and questioned Rhodan with his eyes.

'Yes, he still has a final card up his sleeve – a mutant, unknown to us and whose special talents are still a mystery. This much we could find out from his liberated colleagues. Nobody knows what his speciality is but it seems to be something ghastly. I'm convinced the Supermutant won't be long in playing his last card. That will mean another chance for us – if we're lucky.'

Bell made a face and joined the two men who were sitting at a table. 'So I'm supposed to be your guinea pig again. When do I start?'

'In a week. Tell me, Reggie, what did the presidents think of the parade in their honour?'

'They were duly impressed,' Bell said with satisfaction. 'I'm quite sure they'll suggest starting next week their negotiations for unification of the world. This way *you'll* have something to do, Perry, while I'm busy off in the solar system searching for the firehead.' He rose to leave.

'Firehead?' Mercant was puzzled.

Rhodan explained: 'Bell's a fiend for nicknames. Calls you, for instance, the Terranian Sherlock Holmes, if I'm not mistaken.'

The usually imperturbable Mercant cracked up. But when he recovered from his laughter and flattery, 'Firehead' was still on his mind and he wanted to know what Bell, who had in the meantime departed, had meant by the expression.

'One of his names for the Supermutant,' Rhodan said. 'Sometimes he also calls him Mad Head –'

'Meat head?'

'*Mad* Head. Or Super Sven, short for Svengali. Or Bad Eyes. But I must admit Firehead's the firstime I've heard him use that one.'

No one knew at that moment how appropriate to the future 'firehead' was.

How fiery the path ahead would be.

How prophetic the term 'firehead' – with a pyro-powered twin-headed mutant under the thrall of Hypno!

THE SHIP OF THINGS TO COME

The duel of the mutants has ended with right triumphing over might.

Those whom the mutant master had forced under his hypnotic spell have been for the most part liberated and the prospects are that they can be psychologically reoriented so that they can join the forces of the New Power as valuable collaborators for universal peace and a united front against extra-terrestrial dangers.

But the Supermutant himself was not seized and therein still lies a great danger. For as long as one person remains under the mental control of Clifford Monterny, Earth cannot breathe easy. And one person does – a mutant with pyro-powers!

You'll be enthralled when you read –

THE THRALL OF HYPNO by Clark Dalton

SHOCK SHORT

This story was written before King Kong climbed the Empire State, as you will discover by the reference in it to the Woolworth Bldg. being the greatest skyscraper in New York and the Eiffel Tower the tallest structure in the world. They were – in 1929. Dating from that time, this story won the Second Prize ($75, then a goodly sum) in *Science Wonder Stories*' cover contest. Its author was a young student at the California Institute of Technology at the time. If he is, hopefully, still alive and this story should, as we would like it to, come to his attention, we hope it will not come as too great a shock to him to learn that we have a small reprint check waiting for him if he will contact Forry Rhodan c/o this magabook! Now, on with the story of –

The RELICS
FROM THE EARTH
By
John Pierce

I was to head the expedition! I had been chosen! It was a great honor for a mere youthful graduate terralogist with no great experience and nothing much to his credit. That is, of course, if you do not count my monograph, 'The Last Life Before the Exodus.'

Yes, equipped with two great Goznac discs more than 400 metres in diameter, I was to make a trip to the old Earth, to head the largest archeological expedition in history. I would bring to our museums a few priceless relics of the almost prehistoric era when man lived upon the insect-ridden earth. We were to attempt to save for civilization those two marvels of ancient architecture, the Eiffel Tower, the tallest structure on earth, and the Woolworth Building, the highest skyscraper left standing. That is, we hoped that the decay which made deserts of the formerly great cities had preserved them intact. Many centuries have passed since we migrated to this peaceful little body, Triton, where we are without that terrible scourge, insect life. As I looked about me before departing, I could hardly realize that man once lived upon another and less fertile planet than this, our present home upon Neptune's greatest satellite.

Before many days we were under way. We shouted to the crowd, shot out the immense handling tentacles and waved to the city as we clanged the hatches shut. With our powerful helio-lights we flashed a last farewell, then braced ourselves at our padded station for the force of the acceleration as we rose with unlimited speed.

A few hours later we were far in space. As the acceleration was gradually decreased, almost to zero, all sensation of weight vanished. I made my rounds swinging through the air. I went to the central dome of the pilot house. There I could see only the objects to the side (we were traveling edgewise to avoid meteorites). Around the dome rose the usual will of *consulium*, that marvelously resistant metal discovered by Esfon in 10001, to protect the relatively fragile inner structure; to shield also, the mechanical tentacles. There was little real need of piloting, with the automatic course plotter and steersman working. I looked at the artificial globe of the heavens, seeing on its surface a reflection of all that passed around us. Even as I watched, the surface changed and a small body flashed by, soon to be lost in the distance. Suddenly I saw a familiar bright flash. A muffled clang followed as a portion of the globe went dark for a moment. A tiny meteorite, not fully deflected by the repulsion tubes, had skidded off the wedge-shaped edge of the disc. The ship performed marvelously; and, as I compared it with the uncertain rockets in which my ancestors left the Earth for Venus, I wondered at their courage. To me that feat seemed greater than their later journey, in the first Goznac discs, to our present home.

Three weeks brought us within the attraction of the Earth. The sun blazed in the sky. I could feel the sensation of weight as we slowed down. We intended to remain above the globe for some time, in order to make a careful examination of the surface. Seen through the electro-telescope the Earth was indeed a sorry sight. There was no green thing left on its surface. The insects had killed themselves, worked their own destruction, when they stripped the globe of its vegetation – of the green plants, the only food-producing and air-purifying life upon the earth. What scenes must have enacted when those huge desperate insects with terrible hunger fell upon one another after all other food was gone! The Earth seemed to me but a vast grave.

I observed the cities. Here was our real interest. New York and Paris, the last outposts of man on Earth, were best preserved. In the silent streets of the first, as we hovered about it, I saw the Woolworth Building, the tallest skyscraper remaining. Several thousand miles away was the Eiffel Tower in Paris. In these two structures our objective lay.

After much labor, carried on with the greatest precautions to prevent damage, we ripped the structures from their bases. We were ready to take them where they would serve as imperishable monuments of the days which our race spent on the Earth. It would have taken months to build rigid supports for carrying them but, thanks to the almost human metal arms of our ships, we could take them into space immediately. Making a last inspection of the supporting tentacles on the Woolworth Building, I gave the word. The building was lifted from its severed foundations, supported on a rough cast *consulium* slab held by a tentacle. Cracks appeared in the facing but that was unavoidable and I was justified in my confidence that the steel frame would stand the strain. In the meantime Staner, my assistant, had raised the Eiffel Tower and we started on our long return journey.

As soon as we had the building far enough from the pull of the Earth to permit a great acceleration, my curiosity got the best of me. I donned a space suit of *consulium* air-tight and heat-tight armor and left the disc to inspect the Woolworth Building and its strange contents. As I entered, I thrilled at the thought that here humanity had made a last stand; here it was too, that the survivors of the Great Menace had planned to leave their home forever. Curiously, I wandered about for hours. In one room I stopped over a desk where counsel over humanity's very existence might have been held! I felt a shock.

Later – how long later I do not know – I awoke. I was dazed, lying in a corner of the room in the tower. The spacesuit was bent and I could not move even a leg. The room was littered with a confusion of objects. What had happened?

I crawled painfully to a window, getting there only because of the lack of weight. No discs were visible, no supporting tentacles. The lower part of the building was gone! I was alone in space, adrift in a tiny world of my own! A meteorite had carried away the tower as the disc sped on unknowing! Had they seen my plight? Would Staner realize my fate while there was still a remote chance of his finding me in the vast expanse of space? Was I doomed to die? Such thoughts passed through my mind. I thought of the others, safe in the discs, and envied them. I thought at last of the equipment on my spacesuit, which provided air for me to breathe in airless space. The supply would last only a few hours. If they did not find me – would I die gasping vainly for a last breath? Would I tear open my suit and perish of the cold airlessness of space rather than hang on until strangulation throttled me? In any event, my body would go whirling through space to its tomb, some day to strike a dead planet – some day, with the irony of fate, to reach Neptune, and make for it an eternal satellite.

I looked from the window again. I saw a dot in the distance, rapidly growing larger. The disc! The men had realized my predicament. Surely I was saved!

The disc grew larger – slowly took form. They neared! I could see the tentacles extended. They waved at me. I waved back, knowing that I was observed through the electro-telescope. All the tentacles were extended. Why all? One would have served to hold this small world of mine. The disc drew alongside of the tower. It entwined the tower in a perfect maze of tentacles. Why that precaution? My brain raced. As the power was applied I had a terrible feeling of weight and pressure.

At last I understood the awful truth. My fragment of the building was falling toward some body, gripped by its field of gravitation. The disc was trying to escape, to drag me with it! With enormous effort I turned over. My head lay a foot from a window. Painfully, I reached the window. Resting my face on the frame, I looked out. Below me I saw the immense grayish bulk of the body. Mars! I watched it, fascinated. Minutes passed. Mars rushed toward me! I glanced at the disc. It could not escape. I saw a flash. It was the powerful auxiliary radium rockets. Staner thought to escape by means of the force of their recoil. A feeling of numbness crept over me. The acceleration was too great. What of my friends in the disc? Were they, too –

I awoke on the disc, three weeks later. The fever had gone. Staner was bending over me. Behind him stood the crew. Out of the window I could see the other disc carrying the two buildings. There was a gentle shock as the power went on for a descent. The man lifted me and I could see the landscape of Triton. We were safe and the expedition was a success!

BEFORE THE GOLDEN AGE 1

Isaac Asimov

For many s.f. addicts the Golden Age began in 1938 when John Campbell became editor of Astounding Stories. For Isaac Asimov, the formative and most memorable period came in the decade before the Golden Age – the 1930s. It is to the writers of this generation that BEFORE THE GOLDEN AGE is dedicated.

Some – Jack Williamson, Murray Leinster, Stanley Weinbaum and Asimov himself – have remained famous to this day. Others such as Neil Jones, S. P. Meek and Charles Tanner, have been deservedly rescued from oblivion.

BEFORE THE GOLDEN AGE was originally published in the United States in a single mammoth volume of almost 1,200 pages. The British paperback edition will appear in four books, the first of which covers the years 1930 to 1933.

BEFORE THE GOLDEN AGE 3

Isaac Asimov

In this third volume, Isaac Asimov has selected a
feast of rousing tales such as BORN BY THE SUN
by Jack Williamson, with its marvellous vision of the
solar system as a giant incubator; Murray Leinster's
story of parallel time-tracks SIDEWISE IN TIME; and
Raymond Z. Gallin's OLD FAITHFUL which features
one of science fiction's most memorable aliens –
Number 774.

'Sheer nostalgic delight ... stories by authors
long-forgotten mingle with those by ones who are
well-known, and still writing. A goldmine for
anyone interested in the evolution of s.f.'
Sunday Times

'Contains some of the very best s.f. from the Thirties
... emphatically value for money.'
Evening Standard

A MIDSUMMER TEMPEST

Poul Anderson

'The best writing he's done in years ... his language is superb. Worth buying for your permanent collection.'
– *The Alien Critic*

Somewhere, spinning through another universe, is an Earth where a twist of fate, a revolution and a few early inventions have made a world quite unlike our own.

It is a world where Cavaliers and Puritans battle with the aid of observation balloons and steam trains; where Oberon and Titania join forces with King Arthur to resist the Industrial Revolution; and where the future meshes with the past in the shape of Valeria, time traveller from New York.